LUUANDA

José Luandino Vieira

Translated by Tamara L. Bender with Donna S. Hill

H·E·B

LONDON
HEINEMANN
IBADAN · NAIROBI · EXETER

Heinemann Educational Books Ltd
22 Bedford Square, London WC1B 3HH
P.M.B. 5205, Ibadan · P.O. Box 45314 Nairobi

EDINBURGH MELBOURNE AUCKLAND HONG KONG
SINGAPORE KUALA LUMPUR NEW DELHI
KINGSTON PORT OF SPAIN

Heinemann Educational Books Inc.
4 Front Street, Exeter, New Hampshire 03833, U.S.A.

ISBN 0 435 90222 9

British Library Cataloguing in Publication Data

Vieira, José Luandino
  Luuanda. – (African writers series).
  I. Title   II. Series
  869′.3′4F   P09909.V47L/

ISBN 0-435-90222-9

Set in 11 on 12 pt Bembo
Printed in Great Britain by
Butler & Tanner Ltd
Frome and London

for Linda

Mu 'xi ietu iá Luuanda mubita ima ikuata sonii . . .
'In this our land of Luanda painful things are
happening . . .'

(from a popular story)

Contents

Translator's Preface

Among the Kimbundu-speaking peoples who comprise the majority of the population within a radius of 150 miles of the city of Luanda, the oral story-teller's version of 'once upon a time' was *mu 'xi ietu iá Luuanda* ('in this our land of Luanda'). Angola's principal city for over four centuries, Luanda has held almost mystical dimensions for the African populations living under Portuguese colonial rule. In popular lore it was believed that anything could, and often did, happen in this busy capital city located nearly a third of the way down Angola's long Atlantic coastline. Not surprisingly, Luanda was long a magnet for African urban migrations as well as the principal centre of Portuguese immigration.

In February 1961 when Angolan nationalists attacked prisons and police stations in Luanda, marking the beginning of the war of liberation, Luanda was really two cities, divided by mutual fear and distrust. Despite the Portuguese mythology of a special aptitude for integrating with tropical peoples, Luanda's African and European populations were essentially separate and distinctive communities. Over 150,000 Europeans (nearly half of all Portuguese in the colony) and a small (less than 50,000) educated and acculturated *mestiço* (mulatto) and African elite lived and worked in a central, asphalt city characterized by large, comfortable, red-roofed houses, tall apartment buildings, and a blend of old and new commercial and government edifices. Curving along one side of a small, pretty bay, this basically European city did not lack a tropical flavour for the beautifully lush flora of a humid sun-fed land lined its avenues and shaded its homes.

Surrounding this lovely colonial capital was a ring of *musseques* – sprawling, over-populated slums where roughly half a million Africans (approximately ten per cent of all Africans in Angola by the 1960s) lived in haphazardly constructed shanties of tin, cardboard, mud and wattle which leaned against each other in a precarious balance. Here barefoot naked children with distended bellies played in the dirty rust-coloured sand which was alive with the disease-spreading insects bred by domestic animals and untreated garbage. Lacking electricity and running water the *musseques* did not receive even the most basic sanitary (or social) services usually provided in an urban area.

Although African families were seldom found living in the relative comfort of European and *mestiço* neighbourhoods, Africans did come into the city every morning to provide the cheap domestic services demanded by a colonial society. Private commerce also brought the two populations into contact in the form of tiny shops (*quitandas*) scattered throughout the *musseques* where European or *mestiço* merchants sold dry goods and drinks at an exorbitant profit to their African clientele. In addition a few impoverished European families lived in shanties in one or another of the *musseques*.

After the war of liberation began, life for Angola's African populations became increasingly more difficult. In Luanda the *musseques* began to be subjected to sudden onslaughts of soldiers or police whose noisy jeeps would speed along the dirt paths in the wee hours of the morning and screech to a halt in front of a group of shanties. Sent as search parties by colonial authorities who suspected the *musseque* populations of harbouring nationalist cadres or, at least, nationalist sympathies, these armed intruders would ransack the Africans' meagre belongings. Under orders to confiscate all arms or munitions, they also took anything of monetary or edible value. They would often beat any onlooker who dared to protest and randomly selected one or two to be taken in for more beatings and interrogation about what the Portuguese termed 'suspected terrorist activities'.

* * *

In 1963 José Luandino Vieira, who had grown up among *musseque* children in Luanda, wrote in Kimbundu *Mu 'xi ietu iá Luuanda mubita ima ikuata sonii* – 'In this our land of Luanda painful things are happening', as an introductory quotation for his fourth book, a collection of three stories which he entitled *Luuanda*. He used the Portuguese term *estórias* ('tales') as the book's subtitle, instead of the more traditional Portuguese term *histórias* ('stories'), because he believed *estória* more correctly translated the Kimbundu word *musoso*, defined as a moral story or allegory, fable, narrative, or tale. 'My intent in these narratives,' he explained, 'was to take their structure from oral tradition, employing the stylistic and linguistic characteristics of the popular oral language so that the tales themselves could be told aloud . . .' Written in the mixture of Kimbundu and Portuguese spoken in Luanda's *musseques*, the three tales reveal both the strength and humour of the *musseque* people and their suffering and humiliation.

Not surprisingly very few Portuguese, whether or not they had lived in Luanda, could completely understand the language of Vieira's *Luuanda*. It is a Portuguese whose grammatical structure more closely approximates that of Kimbundu and whose vocabulary is liberally sprinkled with pure Kimbundu and a 'portuguesation' of Kimbundu words, especially in verb formations. Vieira refused to provide a glossary for his book because, as he explained, he wrote his *estórias* for the very people whose language he used, adding that ignorance of *musseque* speech was the problem of the Portuguese colonizer, not his. His use of an introductory quotation in Kimbundu without translation was his ironic imitation of the predilection of Portugal's writers to introduce their books with untranslated, erudite quotations in English or French.

The first edition of *Luuanda* appeared in 1964 while its author was in prison on charges of distributing 'subversive' pamphlets. An activist for the Popular Movement for the Liberation of Angola (MPLA), Vieira spent eleven years in prison, eight of which were in the infamous Tarrafal in the Cape Verde Islands where the Portuguese authorities sent most of those individuals involved in political activities against their colonial regime. A good portion of his literary work was, in fact, written (in secret) while Vieira was in prison and smuggled out, though not published until the Portuguese dictatorship fell in 1974.

In 1965 the Portuguese Writers Society, Portugal's oldest and most prestigious literary association, awarded *Luuanda* its Grand Prize for fiction. This act infuriated the Salazar government which had been preparing to ban Vieira's book. Within a few weeks of the award, the Portuguese secret police raided the Society's headquarters in Lisbon, physically destroyed its offices and officially closed the Society down for the first time in its history. *Luuanda* was now banned from legal circulation and most copies disappeared except for a clandestine edition published in Brazil in 1965 without Vieira's authorization. During the last half of the 1960s and early 1970s, coveted and dog-eared copies of *Luuanda* passed from hand to hand, both in the colonies and among the more enlightened elements in Portugal itself.

In 1972 José Luandino Vieira was released from the Tarrafal prison but sent to Lisbon under a conditional parole. His pleas to be allowed to return to Angola were ignored. A few months after his release, Edições 70, a Lisbon publishing house which employed Vieira as an editor, published the second legitimate edition of *Luuanda*. Both Vieira's release from prison and the publication of his by now famous book marked the beginning and the end of the Portuguese government's proclaimed policy (under Marcello Caetano) of liberalization. Within a few months of its 1972 publication, *Luuanda* was banned again – but not before the reading public had gobbled up every one of the 3,525 copies of this edition. From then on, however, no Portuguese publisher was allowed to print any of his works and Vieira's voice was silenced once more.

In April 1974 a military coup overthrew the fascist Portuguese regime and set the stage for the independence of Portugal's African colonies. Shortly thereafter *Luuanda* was reissued in a third edition. Before the end of 1974 the third edition had sold out and a fourth was published. During those same eight months, three more books by Vieira appeared in print.

As the composition of Angola's transitional government was being worked out during January 1975, José Luandino Vieira and his family returned to his beloved Luanda after an absence of fourteen long years. On December 10, 1975, one month after Angola's Independence was proclaimed in Luanda (November 11), Angola's writers, led by Dr. Antonio Agostinho Neto, President of the newly formed People's Republic of Angola and its most popular poet, issued a proclamation creating the Union of Angolan Writers. It was Luandino Vieira who read the proclamation to the public at the Union's opening session. In September 1977 he was elected as the Union's first Secretary-General. By the end of 1978, under Vieira's dynamic director-ship (he was re-elected Secretary-General on December 29, 1978), the Union of Angolan Writers had published 455,000 copies of 32 different works by Angolan writers and poets. Of these works eight were written by Vieira, including *Luuanda* which was now in its seventh edition, having sold a total of 14,000 copies in Angola alone since Independence.

In this English translation of *Luuanda*, some of the stylistic aspects of its language have, unfortunately, been lost. A literal translation would have made the English incomprehensible. In order to preserve as much of *Luuanda*'s linguistic flavour as possible, however, liberties have been taken with the English language in both phrasing and construction. In addition the reader will note that selected words and phrases have not been translated and are italicized in the text. A glossary has been appended to provide definitions or explanations of the italicized words or passages. Certain proper names will also be found in the glossary.

I would like to express my deep gratitude to José Luandino Vieira for his patient and invaluable assistance, without which this English translation of *Luuanda* would never have been possible.

Finally, I would like to thank Donna Hill, whose persistent belief in the translation helped bring it to fruition and whose sensitivity to the sounds and rhythms of English helped preserve much of *Luuanda's* linguistic flavour.

T. L. Bender
Luanda

GRANDMA XÍXI
AND HER GRANDSON
ZECA SANTOS

For more than two months now the rain would not fall. All around the *musseque* small children of the November grass were covered with red dust spread by the patrol jeeps zooming down streets and alleys all tangled up by the confusion of shanties. This is how it was when Grandma began to feel like in the old days the burning heat and the winds refusing to blow and the neighbours overheard her muttering some rain was going to fall maybe even before two more days passed. And it happened the morning was born with white clouds, lazy at first but later black and crazy, climbing up above the *musseque*. Everyone agreed Grandma Xíxi was right, she warned them before going Downtown that the water was sure to come.

There was rain twice that morning.

At first an angry wind chased after all the clouds making them run from the sea to above the Kuanza River. Then it blew them back again from the Kuanza all the way to the city and the Mbengu River. In back yards and doorways people were wondering if it was a game like so many other days when the clouds gathered as if to rain and then the wind would come and shoo them away. Grandma Xíxi warned them, true enough, and in her old woman wisdom it cost her some to lie, yet only the hot air could be heard somersaulting pieces of paper, leaves and rubbish, making rolls of dust dance in the streets. In all the confusion the women hastened to shut windows and doors and bring the little ones inside the shanties because such a wind like this brings bad luck and sickness, it's a witches' wind.

Tired of this game the wind became more quiet, calm. For a while only the trembling leaves of the *mulemba* and *mandioqueira* trees could be heard with the sad *pírulas* singing about the rain that was to come. Then little by little drops of rain began to fall and it was not even five minutes before the whole *musseque* was singing a song of water on the roof tins; the noise smothered all the people sounds, the mothers fussing at their little ones to

2

come in out of the street, cars spitting mud in the face of the shanties, and only the thunder's deep roar could overpower it. When the first big thunderclap burst above the *musseque*, shivering the weak walls of mud and wattle and loosening boards, cardboards and straw mats, everyone closed their eyes, frightened by the blue brilliance of the lightning born in the sky, a great spider web of fire. The people swore later the searchlamp towers disappeared right in the middle of that blazing flash.

It was like this for a long time.

By noon the rain became lighter even though the sky was still ugly and sneering, all black with clouds. The *musseque* seemed like a village floating in the middle of a lagoon, with canals made by rain and the shanties invaded by the red, dirty water rushing towards the tar roads Downtown or stubbornly staying behind to make muddy pools for mosquitoes and noisy frogs. Some of the shanties had fallen down and the people, not wanting to drown, were outside them with the few things they could save. Beneath the grey sunless sky only the blades of grass were shining a prettier colour, their washed green heads peeking out from the pools of water.

When Zeca Santos flung open the door and in his hurry nearly slipped on the shanty's muddy floor, Grandma let out a faint cry, alarmed at his sudden entrance like some *cipaio*. Zeca laughed but Grandma scolded, 'Ená, child! What're you doing? You think we're dogs, coming in like that? Nothing to tell Grandma who it is? No greeting even?'

'Sorry, Grandma. But it's the rain! I was in a hurry!'

Grandma Xíxi smacked her lips against her teeth with annoyance at the excuse and went on sweeping water into the little back yard. She had got back earlier to the shanty and found everything looking like it was in an ocean: loosened clay slipping from the walls, reeds beginning to show through, and the tin roof so full of holes it could be used for roasting cashews. The water was trying hard to make mud out of the dirt floor and even though Grandma tried with all her might her sweeping could not stop it from running back in. Feeling it was

3

best to give up, she sat down on a box and slowly arranged the *massuica* stones in the driest place to make a fire for cooking lunch.

Outside, as though it had been clinging to Zeca Santos' running steps, the rain was pouring down again thick and heavy on the *musseque*. But now there was no more thunder or lightning, only the sound of water running and falling on more water, calling people to sleep.

'Grandma? Now listen, Grandma ...' Zeca's talking was cautious, gentle. *Nga* Xíxi raised her eyes full of tears from the smoking wet wood.

'What're we going to eat? I'm so hungry. You didn't give me *matete* this morning, Grandma. Yesterday I asked for dinner, but you gave me nothing! I can't live like this!'

Slowly Grandma Xíxi shook her head and her face, thin and aged from many *cacimbos*, began to take on that look people feared. Grandma could burn you better than anyone in the *musseque*.

'*Sukua'*! Is this child ashamed of nothing? You know I told you yesterday there's no money. You know I told you to go on out and get work, even servant's work. I warned you, child, didn't I?'

'But, Grandma, now look! Every day I go out for work. Downtown I walk and walk and walk – and there's nothing! Not even in the *musseque* ...'

'Be quiet! You think I don't know you, eh? Is that the way you think? Good for you! But it's me who's been cooking for you all this time.'

Seemed as if the words were giving her strength, making her young. She got up and stood there in front of her grandson. The boy's large head shrank back; you could see in his eyes he was looking for another, better excuse than on all the other days when Grandma started fussing at him ... you lazy-good-for-nothing-party-boy, forever going around thinking about dances, no respect for your father way off in prison and no one else to bring home the money, how're we going to live now

4

they've fired you at the petrol station all because you slept late, child!?

'Grandma, I swear, I was looking for work.'

'You went on to the whiteman *sô* Souto, did you? I told you to; if you work there we eat lunch on credit! Did you go?'

At Grandma's words Zeca frowned, turning away his thin face. In his belly the angry beast hunger brought was gnawing at the lack of food, two days already. This morning only a cup of coffee, seemed like water, and nothing else, then Grandma almost crying when she shook him off the straw mat with her broom to make him get out and look for work Downtown. When Zeca left she was still muttering, her words full of tears, lamenting, 'There isn't even any *maquezo*, nothing! *Aiuê*, this life! What a stinking life!'

Now, seated again on her box, she blew on the fire. The can of water was boiling but there was nothing for her to put into it.

'But, Grandma, are we going to eat?'

'Eat! ... Eat! ... Ach! ... it's shit we're going to eat! You brought money, did you, child, to buy things to eat? ... Everyday you're at parties, your money from work gone on shirts and now Grandma I want to eat, Grandma what're we going to eat?! Make sense, child!'

She kept fanning the flames in her anger; the wood was burning well now, all crackling and making very little smoke. But Grandma could not be quiet, again she wailed, '*Aiuê!* I told you to go on to *sô* Souto. Maybe if you helped him, he'd give us credit again, who knows?'

'*Sô* Souto? That whiteman *sô* Souto! Just look, Grandma, look!' Zeca was taking off the yellow shirt full of colour and flowers, the shirt that cost him his last money and a big confusion with Grandma. In the dim light of the shanty and the sunless day, across his young narrow back, a long red mark became visible. Grandma got up quickly and passed her old calloused hands along the ugly wound.

'*Aka!* How'd you do that? Zeca? Speak up!'

But he had already put the shirt on again. Facing Grandma

5

Xíxi he pushed her slowly to go and sit on her box. Then setting his long, thin body on the little table he began to talk with sad words, 'Grandma, you told me to go there and I went. Honest! Even with the rain about to fall on me and me getting hungry too...'

Sô Souto had received him well, all friendly and smiling, even put his hand on Zeca's shoulder. 'Of course! For the son of João Ferreira there's always something. And how's Grandmother? No need for her to be embarrassed. Tell her the bill is small, she can come back here again.'

Then he disappeared in the direction of his shop, tucking his belly inside his dirty undershirt, and Zeca Santos let his eyes wander over the petrol pump with the drum and measuring crank; it wasn't automatic like those Downtown, not at all. And the two yellow glass panes, each one marking five litres...

'I swear, Grandma, I didn't do anything, I didn't say anything! I was only asking him for work on the petrol pump, nothing else. Only to eat and maybe even get you credit for food. And he was laughing, he was saying yes sir I was the son of João Ferreira, a good man, and then, Grandma, I didn't even see...' Zeca Santos wanted to cry, his eyes filling up with water, but his anger was choking and hot like the scream from the hippo whip on his back and that great fever dried the water in his eyes, the tears that would not fall. '... he hit me! I don't know why, Grandma! I did nothing! When I ran away he stood there screaming at me he would go to the police and I was a thief like Matias who was always stealing the petrol money when he worked there.'

'*Ach?!* But that boy's in jail now, isn't he?'

'Yes, Grandma. It was *sô* Souto took him to the police. And he was screaming at me I was the son of a terrorist* and he would

---

* *terrorist:* During the war of liberation the Portuguese used this term rather than the word 'nationalist' to describe the Angolans fighting for independence. This usage was symbolic of the refusal of the Portuguese to recognize either the possibility or concept of Angolan nationalism.

go to the police and he had no more food for bandits, no more credit...'

Grandma Xíxi Hengele was a witty old woman who would not be overcome by life, finding humour in each day's gossipings and goings on. Yet now these things she was hearing were too much to believe even though the back of her grandson must be speaking the truth. A whiteman like *sô* Souto, a friend of João Ferreira, how could he be whipping the boy only because he went to ask for work? Hummmm. Maybe Zeca was up to his old tricks; it was best to get the whole truth.

'Now listen to me, Zeca! You took from him maybe? You did something with those clothes he got in that shop? Maybe you were just looking?...' Cautious, with all the shrewdness and wisdom of her years, Grandma Xíxi began to test her grandson, asking questions that seemed to wander but were meant to discover if he was speaking a lie. Zeca would have none of it; he jumped up from the table, his ragged shoes making a soft noise on the muddy floor, and screamed in rage to defend himself, 'Dammit, Grandma, I'm no thief! I didn't steal anything! All I wanted was work, I swear it!'

Big sobs and the white tears running down his thin face, his head now bent over the table was hidden in his arms, his body trembling and trembling with the pain of the wrong done him, with the rage hunger brought, hushed Grandma's tongue.

Outside the rain began to fall more fine and slow, just like a *cacimbo* night. Many people were outdoors now and the little ones were playing with boats made of ruined matting and duck feathers in the pools of the *musseque*. Together with the crackling of the burning wood and the singing of the water in the tin can, Zeca's sobs filled the small shanty with a melancholy that little by little began to reach into Grandma and make her old head rock back and forth, back and forth, thinking such a life, no food, no work, grandson crying, maybe this time he was truthful. But then Zeca wasn't getting much more sensible, when he earned money on that job where they fired him, he only wanted shirts, he only wanted fancy pants, he only wanted red socks, even when she warned him to save just a little money – save? Hah! He would shout it was him doing the earning, and those parties and more parties and getting up late and rushing out until one day he got fired. In the middle of all these thoughts a great tenderness crept into her tired old heart, the desire to lay him in her lap like times so long ago, times of a thin, whining little boy. Quietly, to hide the wanting that filled her, Grandma Xíxi went to unwrap the package she brought from Downtown.

There was no rain at all now, only a fresh wet wind shaking drops from the leaves and making small waves in the muddy pools of water. The loosened roof tins clinked slowly with the blowing. Still tearful Zeca Santos raised his head at the sound of the paper being unwrapped under the table, at the sight of Grandma's bent shoulders and her thick, shoeless feet spreading into the red muddy floor. Everything before him seemed clearer, lighter, without so many shadows; the pain in his stomach was there no longer, it only felt fresh, empty, as if nothing was left, it was a void like the shanty was becoming. And Grandma's gentle look as she unwrapped the newspaper in front of him seemed further and further away until it was almost a shadow.

'Zeca, look here, child . . . don't these things I'm going to cook look like little manioc roots? And here's this orange, see this, what I got for you?'

With all these things in front of him and Grandma's smile full of love and sadness, Zeca Santos suddenly felt an old shame, a shame that always made him want the colourful shirts, the trousers only sô Jaime knew how to make, a shame that kept him from accepting food like that morning when Maneco wanted to give him half a sandwich and he gave it back. Now the shame filled him and he shut his eyes as hard as he could, put his hands over them so he would not see what he knew, would not feel, would not think anymore about Grandma's bent old body weary from life and many cacimbos, rummaging beneath the rain with her dry knotted hands in the dustbins

8

Downtown. The nearly rotten oranges – only a little could be saved from each – and even worse those small red manioc roots, Grandma was trying to fool him, she wanted to boil them to put an end to the beast gnawing in his stomach.

Zeca jumped up not knowing what he was doing, his head empty of thoughts. He pushed Grandma Xíxi and ran out before the tears could emerge again in his eyes, shouting with a hoarse voice over and over like he was crazy, 'They're dahlias, Grandma! They're flowers, flower roots, Grandma!'

The door, swollen from the rain, did not fit back into its frame. It slammed hard once, twice, then began creaking, softly moaning Zeca's departure. In the middle of the darkened shanty, smoky from the dying fire, Grandma Xíxi remained staring after her grandson, clutching the dahlia roots in her trembling hands, not even aware of her head nodding from side to side like the puppet in a lottery window.

*   *   *

... Madame Cecília de Bastos Ferreira, seated in a woven palm chair at the door of her house, is enjoying the fresh five o'clock breeze but the flies will not leave her alone. It is December and very hot; her man, Bastos Ferreira, a mulatto from an old family of exiled Portuguese, has been gone now twice fifteen days to trade in the interior not far away, making his rounds on foot with his *monangambas* – he didn't like the litter, said a man does not travel on the backs of other men.

The sun slides lazily behind the hill of the Fortress and all the Coqueiros neighbourhood is covered by a powder of light making the sea in the distance seem like a looking glass. But the flies are too many and suddenly the voice of Cecília Ferreira, *nga* Xíxi to her friends and neighbours, causes confusion among the girls in the house who are cutting, sewing and ironing the cloths and dresses to be sold in the market.

'Madía! Madí'é! Come here!'

So *nga* Xíxi, Madame Cecília, living in Coqueiros in a house

9

with its own little garret, with girl disciples★ who learn sewing and cooking from her, and with a cloth market trade, sits outside facing the street, fat and sweaty, feeling the sweetness of the breeze which Maria now fans for her.

The afternoon is coming to an end, people are passing by on the way to their homes and respect for the Bastos Ferreira family can be seen in their greetings, their smiles, the bowing of their shoulders as they ask, '*Nga* Xíxi, how are you? You feeling well? And your man?'

'Good afternoon, Madame Cecília, enjoying the fresh air?'

There's even Abel, that rascal whiteman from the Customs House who comes all attentive and self-seeking to kiss the hand of shining black skin, 'My sincere compliments to you from your most humble admirer!'

Like sea shells her white teeth laugh. She rolls her eyes at him but not in anger or scorn – there's a hidden satisfaction in the movement of her pretty eyes – and then she points to the straw mat, her words almost serious, 'Go play with little João, Abel! If Bastos Ferreira would hear your words, Abelito, you'd have to change your underwear!'

And smacking her teeth she sends him off because conversation with that man can be a danger if it keeps going, everyone knows that. Inside the house there is laughter and singing again as the girls noisily go back to their work; they had stopped because this was the time they always liked to listen to *nga* Xíxi making fun of the man from Customs.

★ *disciples:* In Angola the disciples represented a kind of informal educational system whereby the more wealthy and well-established African and mulatto families in urban areas would invite the children of relatives or friends from the interior to come to the city to live with them and learn 'civilized ways'. The children would learn how to sew, cook, tend a home, care for younger children, 'good manners', etc., all patterned after the Portuguese way of life. This system also provided the urban families with a kind of unpaid domestic service. According to Vieira the development of this system of disciples was a kind of transition from the old master–slave relationship since previously these urban families had used domestic slaves.

10

Dona Cecília goes on watching little João, a quiet boy with large almost motionless eyes. Over Coqueiros the breeze of the day's end spreads the colours of the sun fleeing into the sea; it is a great red sun that swells and burns the colours of the houses, the green of the trees, the blue of the sky...

... Seated on the wet floor in the doorway of the shanty, *nga* Xíxi Hengele – as they call her in the *musseque* because she talks in a way that makes some people laugh and confuses all the rest – mutters as a narrow ray of sunlight escapes the clouds to fall on her old thin face. Grandma blinks her eyes, her body feels limp, her mouth bitter, head heavy. Then she remembers, she was day-dreaming; a sad smile twists the lines on her face, 'Nga Xíxi...Madame Cecília!...Why remember now?' She laughs a dull spent laugh, hoarse from the tobacco of the little cigars smoked lit end in. '*Auá!* Maybe it's the maniocs I ate.'

True her belly is aching. Only watery coffee for days and then all of a sudden she cooked those potatoes and ate every one, maybe that's what's made her sick. Their taste wasn't exactly manioc or even sweet potato, those tastes Grandma knows well, but she refuses to remember the words of her grandson when he left angry at lunch time. 'No!' she sighs. 'It's not my time to die and I'm not hungry now anyway.'

But still those images which came to her in her dream do not want to let go, they cling to her in memories unwilling to leave – nothing was lacking at home, plenty of food and clothes and no need to talk about money. It continues to eat at her even now, no longer being Madame Cecília Bastos Ferreira, and Grandma doesn't resist, doesn't struggle, what for? She lets those tattered bits of times passed play in her head, bringing regret, sorrow, and just goes on repeating very softly as if to excuse herself, 'So, it's life. The Lord has his own reasons ... only He knows...'

A little sunlight coming through the clouds brings a warmth fresh from the rain. Along the wires crisscrossing the *musseque* flocks of *piápias* perch, carelessly forgetting the children's slingshots. Already sparrows are hopping about – the sparrow doesn't know how to walk so that's how he moves over the wet ground to catch the *jingunas* to fill his craw. On the younger branches of the *mulembas*, *plim-plaus* and *rabos-de-junco* are singing about their capture of the figs. Wasps zoom crazily out of their nests in the cashew trees; the *gumbatetes* take advantage of the mud to build their houses. Hens and chicks had already ventured out of the shanties long ago when the rain was still young and stirred up all the ground where grasshoppers and termites and ants live. Only the dogs stayed in the doorways, curled up in holes, making good use of the cool dirty sand.

But Grandma doesn't feel these sounds of life around her. There's the blowing of the wind, the clinking of roof tins, the singing of water still running in some places and, above everything, mingling with all the other sounds, the buzzing voices of *musseque* people talking and laughing just as if without the living of people the rest could not be heard at all, even the sweet music of birds and branches and water would be silent. For Grandma all of this is old, very old, she has known it all through her life, every year, every *cacimbo*, every rain; but now her belly hurts her, her head is getting heavier and heavier, her body cold. She does not even have the will to go back inside the shanty but lets herself stay just as she is, sitting down, flies resting on her black cloths, her mouth gasping in the fresh air, eyes half-closed.

'Good afternoon, Grandma Xíxi. How are things with you?'

She opens her eyes, wanting to smile but the sun on her face doesn't let her. She recognizes *nga* Tita. 'Ah! Good, thank you, child. How's Gregório?'

Nga Tita lowers her head, shrugs her shoulders; then answers with more courage, 'Same thing, *nga* Xíxi! Always the same.'

Old Xíxi leans her hands against the wall and her friend helps her get up, slow and careful; her neighbours know how the rheumatism waits for these cool wet days to attack.

'*Aiuê!* The life of the poor!'

'That's right, Grandma. *Sukuama!* You know there's no one to tell me when Gregório can get out or anything! I was talking to the boss man down there, I swore my man's no terrorist, no sir, always he's slept in bed with me so how could he be with the fighters and all these other things they say?'

Grandma Xíxi sighs, her belly hurting, paining her. 'Yes I know, child. But that's the way of things. The whites never believe...'

'*Ach!* That boss man answered maybe my man sleeps with me but he's the one who knows him. You believe that, Grandma! You believe such a thing?... Well, time to be going. When I'm coming back, I'll stop again to talk with you.'

'Thank you, child. But tell Grandma Xíxi...' Her quiet eyes open wide as her voice begins with these words. Grandma's curiosity – she has to know everything about everything, has to have her say, to come right out with her thoughts – makes her ask, '... you going far?'

'To *sô* Cristiano, Grandma.'

'To do what in *sô* Cristiano's?'

'You don't know? Ay, you don't know! His wife gave him a girl!'

'*Ená!* Another? Damn! Girls is all that man can make!'

'That's right, Grandma. But he says it's her fault. He wanted to beat her the same day the little one came out! Would you believe it?!'

Grandma Xíxi laughs, this conversation makes her old weary laugh seem young. The small eyes, hidden deep in their sockets, are blinking and her whole face, lit up by the newly shining sun, seems like it's covered with palm oil. *Nga* Tita comes closer to tell her how the girl was born fair, honest, Grandma, born white, white like the daughter of an *ngueta*; fact is, if she wasn't knowing her friend Domingas well she could be thinking maybe some whiteman went to the wrong shanty door...

Grandma laughs, clapping her hands and closing her eyes in delight, then doubles over to laugh even harder. And while *nga* Tita is saying goodbye with a chuckle and walking away on the wet dirty sand towards Rangel, Grandma finds her old courage again, even her cheerfulness, though hunger still gnaws

13

at her belly, and smug and playful she shouts, 'Listen, child! *Mu muhatu mu 'mbia! Mu tunda uazele, mu tunda uaxikelela, mu tunda uakusuka ...'*

*　　*　　*

The two of them were walking along, quiet now after much conversation during lunch. Maneco was puffing on a cigarette, his hands in the pockets of his oil-covered monkey suit, while Zeca Santos was looking in every window pane and into the eyes of the passing girls, enjoying the vanity that yellow flowered shirt gave him. Slowly, at his friend's side, he could feel a fire growing bigger and bigger in his stomach, spreading through his blood, climbing to his head and making a fine cloudy mist before his eyes. But it was better like this. He forgot the beast in his belly, he even forgot Grandma and the roots she wanted to give him for lunch, he forgot the work he couldn't find ...

It was not yet four o'clock and with no special place in mind they continued along the street of the Catonho-Tonho Company towards the sea. Zeca Santos had caught up with his friend, finding him still at work; rainy days brought many cars into the service station and wanting to put in some time for a friend, Maneco was leaving late. That's why it was three o'clock before Maneco came out for lunch. Straight away they started carrying on about the dance last Saturday and that fight over Delfina. Maneco praised Zeca, 'That was a great flip, man! Damn! Everybody was talking about it!'

Praised like this, Zeca Santos straightened up his thin body, his flappy ears were hot, burning – how he hated those ears, the girls liked to tease him and only when he began to talk would the music of his words make them forget. He stole a look at his yellow shirt and vainly continued walking with his friend to the little *quitanda* where they could eat.

The moment they went into the shop and Maneco greeted *sô* Sá ordering two lunches, out came the lie; with no thought in his head, not even hearing the hungry beast crying out in his stomach, that lie cost Zeca. It was shame talking with words he was sorry for later, 'Huh! Two lunches? I just ate, Maneco.' And even though Maneco said nothing, Zeca heard himself repeating, 'I swear! I ate so much I'm full!'

Ay! but there was a good hot smell coming from Maneco's soup, the spoon going up and down, the noise of the car-washer's lips sucking in the bean puree. How could Zeca Santos bear it all, so anxious to hide the saliva he kept swallowing, gulping down? And then came the *quitande*, that good-smelling yellow bean stew. Brother Maneco ate and smiled but not even his hunger after long hours of work stopped him talking about girls and dances and the motor bike that he was maybe going to buy at the station. Zeca just watched his friend's teeth, yellow from the palm oil, his lips shining with the fat, and he hardly said a word; he, Zeca Santos, who knew nothing else but stories about parties and girls! Finally his hunger was too great and when the bananas came he could stand it no longer. With a hollow voice he spoke up, wanting to pretend it was nothing at all, 'Oh all right then, maybe a banana. There wasn't any time for fruit ... you know, Maneco, with the bus...'

The words stuck in his mouth. He had already told Maneco he came on foot, that he liked to walk after a rain. He glanced up to see if he would be caught out by this lie. Distracted by the food, Maneco was not really listening and Zeca Santos was able to swallow two bananas in a hurry, without chewing them up at all ... Ah, and that glass of wine is what really helped to lull the moan in his belly. Feeling calmer, relieved, no more throbbings in his stomach, the saliva easier in his mouth, he too began talking about girls, Delfina, dances...

Outside the sun had already melted away the last pieces of cloud and was peeking out from behind the leaves of the trees grown full in their old age. Slowly crossing the pebbled street, Maneco smoking, Zeca Santos happy with the wine in his belly, they let their feet carry them past the Central Post Office to the breakwater, to the palm trees and benches of the broad avenue alongside the sea where on Sundays or in the evenings the white people from Downtown come to stroll with their families. Sitting down facing the sea, dark and reddened by the rain waters, Maneco turned the conversation.

'Ya got anything yet?'

'Nothing, Maneco.' Zeca kept away from telling about *sô* Souto's whip, much better to keep quiet about that story. 'More than a week now I'm looking for work and there's nothing!'

Maneco lit another cigarette then spat into the water, 'And that one from the newspaper. Did ya go?'

'Not yet.'

'Better go and try today, ya never know . . .'

'Oh they're not going to take me. I'm too thin and they say "office and warehouse" in that newspaper. You know already it means heavy work.'

Maneco opened the clipping and read the ad aloud, slowly, looking at each letter – he didn't have much schooling and reading fast was hard for him. When he finished he leapt to his feet like a cat and playfully slapped Zeca on the back, 'Let's go, kid!'

Maneco was always calling him kid when he was going to help Zeca with something; knowing this by now, Zeca smiled. At his friend's side, feeling his head begin to spin and the brilliant sea tremble, he said, 'I'll go myself, Maneco. All right? You said you still had to help your friend and do some more of his hours at the station.'

Maneco just grabbed his arm, to help him cross the street, then before leaving he advised, 'Now listen, Zeca. If ya don't get anything, come on over to the station. Then, if ya really want, I can take ya to Sebastião to do cement work tomorrow. But it's up to you, ya know!'

Twilight was coming and the sun burned its way towards the sea, leaving not one cloud in the blue sky and attacking the Downtown, defenceless without trees. Zeca Santos' stomach was not complaining now but the heat was all over his body, making his feet itch so that he walked fast through all the people, his yellow shirt turning this way and that as he tried not to bump

16

into them. He approached the place of the ad with courage, already arranging in his head the words, the reasons – he would talk about his old grandma, it didn't matter what the work was they might want to give him, he would take it . . .

But at the entrance he stopped, the old fear once again in his heart. A huge glass door faced him, letting him see inside where everything was shining, threatening. At a table near the door he was watched by a boy, perhaps older than him, in a well-starched khaki uniform. In a glimpse Zeca Santos saw himself in the glass and the yellow flowered shirt, his pride and glory with the girls around, all mussed up from the rain, his old blue trousers too many times washed white at the knees, and he felt the sharp cold from the black stone of the entrance through the holes in his ragged shoes. Every bit of courage fled from him now, even the words he had dared to think up to tell of his will to work, and in his belly the beast began its work again, gnawing, gnawing. Tentatively, afraid of smudging it, he pushed the glass door open and went in, moving towards the big counter. But he didn't have time to go far. A tall thin man stood in front of him, looking at the notice in his hand. Zeca was about to speak but the man just shoved him to the errand boy's table.

'Yes, I know, I know. Don't say anything! You've come about the ad, right? Over here. Xico, oh Xico!'

The boy in the uniform came running with a notebook and pencil, then stopped in front of him, expectantly. The thin man looked carefully into Zeca Santos' eyes and suddenly burst out with a lot of questions like he wanted to make Zeca nervous: where did he work? what did he do? how much did he earn? if he was married who was the family? was he an *assimilado*? did he have a letter of good behaviour from other bosses? and lots of other things giving Zeca Santos no time to answer at all. Finally, when Zeca was trembling from the cold office air and the emptiness eating at his belly and voices fading farther and farther away the man loomed up before him eyeing his shirt and his tight trousers with suspicion and distrust.

'Listen here, boy, where were you born?'

'Where you born?' repeated the errand boy.

'Catete, boss.'

The man whistled and taking his glasses away from his tired eyes, he struck the table, 'From Catete, huh? *Icolibengo?* Uppity, lazy good-for-nothing thieves! And what's more, terrorists now! Get out of here, you son-of-a-bitch. Out, son of a whore! I don't want Catetes in here!'

Zeca Santos did not know how it was he left so quickly without bumping into the glass door. The man's face was terrifying, all red like he was crazy or drunk, and he was shaking his finger, threatening, yelling insults; people passing by bumped into the silent startled boy while the man in the door kept on shouting, '*Icolibengo*, huh! Bastard! You come around here again and I'll split your balls!'

Suddenly, seeing everyone on the pavement begin to stop and ask what was going on, fear warned Zeca like a signal in the dark that had been asleep and was now awakened in the midst of danger and with hunger putting red stripes before his eyes, he ran off along Alfandega Street to escape in the throng of people in Mutamba.

*   *   *

The soursop tree stood near the street, on the land where long ago the old folks' home had been.

So solitary was that soursop tree with the large many-windowed houses gazing on it, surrounding it from every side, that it seemed like something bewitched. No longer ever watered, it lived only from the rain and continually struggled with black smoke from the trucks in their comings and goings to the port. How was it that the tree still had the courage and strength to give good shade, to grow its dirty green leaves, even to ripen the soursops which always held the freshness of cottony flesh, the pleasure of spitting far the black seeds and even of tearing off the thorny skin? Only farther above in the gullies of the Florestas were there more trees. Here, alone and brave, it sheltered in its shadow blackened *massuicas* where the *monangambas* from coffee warehouses, apprentices from workshops, and even city workers when they came with their shovels and pickaxes to tear up the belly of the streets, cooked their meals.

At that hour of almost five o'clock, the leaves were rustling softly and the spreading shade was good, fresh like water from the clay jug. Seated on the smoke-blackened stones, Zeca Santos was waiting for Delfina, staring anxiously at the factory door. He had made a date with the girl – that day she was to ask if she could leave early and they would meet; Zeca wanted to pick up again the playful words of Saturday's party. Delfina had danced very well with him and later when the band burst out with the song of the *Kabulu*, no one else could catch them, the dance was almost theirs alone – everyone had stopped to watch them, so vain and pleased with themselves. From that sprang the fight with João Rosa: he was always chasing after the girl, wanting her for himself, but that night Zeca Santos, seeing the satisfaction in Delfina's eyes, would have fought everyone. He was the lucky one, not João Rosa because he wore glasses and the light outside was dim. He missed the punch at Zeca's face, and with no trouble at all Zeca caught hold of his arm and threw him into the dirt.

But even though Zeca had won that fight, the mulatto continued to call for Delfina at home in his little car and often picked her up at work when it was dark. Zeca got furious when he thought about the silence and the car hiding in the dark and maybe that bastard daring to touch his girl's legs, even other things ... that car was helping him.

Zeca made up his mind that day. Maybe it was the glasses of wine at lunch and one more with Maneco after they talked to Sebastião, maybe it was the promise of a job. The truth was that now he saw everything more confidently, light-heartedly almost. Even without his realizing it, the thought of having money to send his shoes to be mended and of maybe getting some new trousers got all mixed up with the image of Delfina, her smile and her talk, her light sweet leaning against him during the tangos, at the parties ...

Sebastião had received them well; Maneco was a friend. Big, almost bald, the man talked to Zeca Santos with a deep voice, he even felt his arms. Then he spat, but Maneco was there to help.

'Enough, Mbaxi! The boy needs work.'

Sebastião the Monkey-Face – *Polo ia Hima* the men would shout while lying down in the shadow of the trees waiting for the trucks – warned him the work would be heavy; come on at seven, off at six, and all day long suffering the cement bags on your shoulders, loading the trucks, only resting for some fried fish on bread. And the worst is the dust all the time, even if you put a cloth over your mouth it gets in just the same.

'And you, boy, you're not strong! Don't want to fool you.'

Zeca Santos mumbled something, not even he knew what; you had to respect the man with his broad chest and arms like tree trunks and a voice as thick as the huge legs bulging out of trousers torn short over his knees.

Pointing to all the others sitting or lying around, Sebastião roared the great laugh of a bossman, then lowered his voice, 'You going to take work away from one of these men?! ... Oh, all right! I choose anyway when the trucks come and you go with me.'

Maneco held out his hand to say goodbye but the man didn't take it. He kept on laughing and laughing; then spoke again. Zeca Santos did not see why the man laughed like that but the words startled him, 'Them fellas usually pay forty *escudos* for this job. Used to be sixty a day but with more and more people coming 'round here to work lately, the bastards take advantage.'

He looked around, quiet now and careful, eyes glittering from a face squashed in by his large jaw. 'And every day ten of that forty's for me, okay?'

Zeca Santos opened his mouth but Maneco was already complaining, '*Ená*, Mbaxi! Just look at the boy ... and besides he's got an old one at home to feed.'

'And me? I don't have any seven children? How'm I going to

feed them, eh? Dress them? If he don't take it there's men here who's going to give me as much as half if I let'm load the cement.'

Maneco still wanted to protest, to make it less, five *escudos* was enough to take out, the boy would have to work hard, struggle, he wasn't used to it, he deserved the pay ...

'That's the point!' he laughed. 'That's it! The little one's not going to keep at it; I'll be loading the rest!'

In the midst of such a laugh that it shook the muscles under his shirt, he turned his back on them and went to lie down again under the old tree where they had found him, still shouting, 'Six o'clock, better be here. If not, someone else will. And it's still ten for me!'

Maneco gestured obscenely towards him and for some time Zeca Santos, a weight on his heart, didn't even feel like talking until he said goodbye to his friend and reached the door of the tobacco factory to meet up with Delfina.

Now with the girl at his side, he forgot all about Sebastião *Polo ia Hima*. In fear of the approaching night, the heat of the day was withdrawing and a wind still fresh from the morning rain slapped Delfina's dress against her strong legs, her firm body. The green grass seemed to invite them from all around and wet like it was it tickled Zeca Santos' feet, getting inside his ragged shoes. He walked without speaking, not knowing anymore what to say to Delfina, everything invented under the soursop tree, even those sweet words born so freely in the mood of parties, now refused to come out. Along the path he heard cicadas singing in the trunks of the acacia trees, flower-wrapped branches dancing in the wind, leaves whispering of lovers, all the noise of the humming birds, sparrows, and *plim-plaus* chasing after the rain bugs. Delfina walked along with a teasing smile and finally it was she who interrupted the silence.

'*Ená!* We meet and you don't even have two words for me?'

'Oh, Fina. The words I have you know already.'

'Huh? I do? When did I hear them? Anyway, have you got a job now?'

Zeca did not answer. Delfina was always after him with these conversations about a job and even when he was trying to make fun of that João Rosa, half-blind and I don't know what else, the girl would snap back, 'You, you're just jealous! That boy works, he's got his own car, he even talks about marrying me.'

He liked Delfina so much, even wanted her to know all about his life, but then how was he going to tell her what was going on all these days of looking for work? Or even talk about that job of loading cement on the dock, that *monangamba* work? She would never accept that, she would leave him that minute, right there in the middle of the ravines. And to say that he had no job, that he had not found work, was worse. Delfina went on talking and you could hear in her voice it was just to make him mad – she was saying João Rosa had already promised to talk to the boss about her moving up to the office and that she should be going to night school and that he wanted to marry her if she would accept him and lots of other things, only to irritate Zeca Santos. They were hurting him inside, he felt sadness, shame; he liked the girl, it's just that he had no luck, and what's worse a full-time job is no easy thing to find. He thought the afternoon was going to be nice now with their meeting; what a pity Delfina decided to trouble him like this. He took hold of her arm, carefully, and lowering his voice he talked the way he knew best.

'Now listen, Fininha. You forgot Saturday, what you said, eh? What're you getting angry for? And why talk all that nonsense about good-for-nothing Rosa, what for? I don't get jealous, what're you thinking of? Now I got my own job down there at the station with Maneco . . . and anyway you know you saw Marcelina chasing after me at the dance . . .'

'What? That sneak?! *Sukuama!* What's she hanging around for?' Delfina shut up right away. Zeca's smile was before her, a smile she liked and hated at the same time, it made his face look like a cat's when it plays with the rat.

Slowly and with all the experience he had, Zeca turned her off the path and they walked a little way through the grass, butterflies and grasshoppers jumping all around. Sitting down under a big acacia tree, red with flowers, Zeca pulled on Delfina's waist, showing her only those laughing eyes of the mis-

22

chief-making little boy she liked so much. But she shook him off, pushing away his bold hands and, smoothing her dress, she sat down her way, close by, then pulled the colourful calico above her knees, holding it beneath her strong thighs.

For a time Zeca Santos lay there sucking on a piece of grass, not saying anything. Then he began to inch towards Delfina, watching her with honey friendly eyes. The girl didn't say a word but let his head lie in her lap; it was good to feel his weight, the warmth of him against her belly, his flappy ears showing off the shape of his head, eyes full of happiness. Unable to stop them, she let her hands put downy caresses on his tight hair and the warm skin of his neck, and Zeca sighed, 'Ah, Fina, my love. If you go with that João Rosa anymore, I don't know what I'll do.'

'I won't anymore, Zeca, I swear! It's only you I love, only you, you know that.'

He smiled; it was sweet to feel those words, the caresses, the warmth of her hands all over his skin. Nothing was left in his body, not the hunger gnawing in his stomach nor the wine making things hazy and light, only a blush more pleasing than the breeze rustling the tiny green leaves of the acacias, stirring the flowers until their red and yellow petals fell, making a rain of coloured tissue all around them.

'Now you've found yourself a good job, Zeca, you won't be sleeping so late, will you?'

'No, Fina!'

'If you want me to get you up in the morning, I can knock on the window.'

Zeca smiled again, happy with her friendship. 'No, Fininha, it's all right. From now on I'm going to have sense, I swear it!'

'It's time, Zeca. *Sukuama!* I can't be loving you if you're not going to show some more sense!'

Delfina's large clear eyes were showing the lie in those words but Zeca didn't see them. His head in her lap, he was feeling shame, feeling an urge to tell the girl only the truth like she deserved, yet he was certain that saying anything now would lose her for sure, especially when she found out he only had a *monangamba*s' job. His head began to pound with these thoughts. And even worse there was still João Rosa with his car and his flattering talk all meant to steal her away.

His pain became great . . . then the gnawing in his belly seized him again, taking away the last good things of the afternoon. Everything began to swirl around making him dizzy, his stomach churn, a sour bitter saliva in his mouth, all his insides begging to throw up the bananas and the wine that had soured them. Suddenly, with the eyes of a frightened animal and hands reaching out in defence, he sought Delfina's body clutching at a last refuge against the hurt of that day and all the days before. Maddened by the fear of vomiting, he felt her small breasts pressed beneath his fingers, then her thick black thighs no longer covered by the dress.

The cicadas stopped their song and a humming bird fled from the tree where it was sucking flowers; Delfina slapped his face with all the strength she had and Zeca, thin and unsteady, tumbled against the trunk of the acacia.

Nearly in tears and grasping at her dress where his fingers had torn away the buttons, Delfina spat at Zeca all the foul words that came into her head, 'You thinking I'm from your family, is that it? That I'm one of those lay-down-in-the-grass-pay-fifty-*escudos*-come-sleep-with-me? You think that? You stinking, rotten, no-good bum, you've got no shame! You skinny pimp for your grandmother!'

But Zeca Santos no longer knew what was happening. Full of the vomit gathering in his belly, he pushed his hands against himself trying to take a deep breath, to get up, but again Delfina shoved him against the trunk of the acacia. Then running away through the grass, butterflies and grasshoppers jumping from her angry feet, cicadas hushed by her words, she kept screaming as long as Zeca could hear, 'No-good bum! Go fuck yourself! A man only gets in here on my wedding day, got that? On my wedding day, in bed, not in the grass like animals, you skinny . . . bastard!'

From the convent school came the echo of the afternoon bell as the sun, huge and red, descended into the sea. Blowing playfully through the tree trunks, the wind brought to his stinging ears Delfina's scream from the bottom of the hill far below where only the pretty colours of her calico dress could be seen through the leaves. 'Not even ashamed, you shit? So skinny you look like a canoe pole. You're even pitiful!'

As he vomited, Zeca Santos was not aware of the stubborn happiness that wanted to be born, to burst from those words Delfina spoke without knowing why anymore.

*   *   *

With the twilight blending into the silent darkness of the shanty, Grandma Xíxi feels her grandson approaching, pushing the door open more gently than he ever did before. His tall, thin figure outlined in the doorway with the light from outside at his back, Zeca had to open his eyes wide to get used to the dark and he walked in with care.

'Grandma? Where are you? Grandma?'

Lying on the straw mat, Grandma moaned and her grandson ran to the corner where she was covered up, trembling.

'What is it, Grandma? Say something! You sick or what?'

'*Aiuê* this life! *Aiuê* my belly! I'm going to die!'

Zeca went back to the door and opened it to let in the light that was dying with the day. The brightness of the searchlamps, whose large eyes peer out above the shadows of all the *musseques*, entered afraid into that ugly darkness. Grandma leaned herself against the wall, a blanket covering her legs and stomach.

'Now then, child,' she sighed, 'tell Grandma ...'

Her grandson knew these words meant the same as all the other days, knew the reason for Grandma always asking, wanting to know if he found work, if he finally earned something to eat with. And there in front of her he was ashamed to talk about the job, kind of work for a *monangamba* from the docks, and what's more having to divide his wages with the bossman. It was better to keep his mouth shut, not talk about these things, just go to work, get the money, buy things to eat, then give Grandma a lie about some other job.

'Nothing yet, Grandma. I looked all over, nothing! Brother Maneco even helped me ... it's just my bad luck.'

'You eat, child?'

'Huh? What was there to eat? Nothing, Grandma.'

'*Aiuê* my belly! You were right, but I was so empty I had to eat them.'

She went on and on with her usual complaints that he didn't have any sense and if he did have none of this would be happening, that's the way it is, when a person gets old, they're finished! The young ones think they're an old rag to throw out. A person gets hungry, eats whatever comes along and then when they're asleep these belly aches attack them and burn them inside worse than *jindungo*, worse even than fire ...

Zeca Santos listened without hearing, his head full of Delfina and the pain of her rejection; how could he ever undo all those things that had happened so suddenly without his even meaning them to. He bet the girl would not stand any more of his talk, even if he excused himself by saying he was sick, she wouldn't believe it, she would call him a liar, a good-for-nothing; and a stubborn melancholy reached into him. His eye swollen red from her slap was throbbing, blinking, making two of everything he saw. But Grandma went on.

'I knew it! I warned you, child. I warned you about going to mass on Sunday. Father Domingos asked about you and it was me had to make excuses about you being sick.'

'*Sukuama!* Father Domingos ... he's going to give me food? Give me work, Grandma?'

The pain from the swollen eye angered Zeca. He began to take off his yellow shirt quickly, almost tearing it, and with that Grandma started in at him again. 'Good! So now you're going to tear it, is that it? Ate up all the money on that party-boy shirt and now you tear it! *Aiuê* this life, these children have no sense, no respect for their old ones.'

Zeca Santos wanted to calm her and besides his head was beginning to hurt. 'But, Grandma, now listen! Don't start nagging me about any old thing like that. So I was sleeping, I didn't go to mass, so what?'

Grandma Xíxi almost jumped to her feet, and not quite able to stand she leaned against the wall. 'So what? So what? Child, you can ask and not remember everyday you're after me with: "Grandma, food? Grandma, where's my *matete*? Grandma, we going to eat?" You remember? *Ach!* ... and Father Domingos, it's him can get you a job!'

'Piss on that! I don't need a job sweeping the church!'

'Shut your mouth, child, and don't be talking about church things like that!'

Zeca Santos didn't answer back, he already knew at such times it didn't help at all to go on talking with Grandma. If he said anything else, they would only be getting mad at each other. His heart ached from the misery of that day and his wounded eye stung, throbbing and swollen; but what made him suffer even more was the fear Delfina would not forgive him, even though it was not really his fault she would be exchanging him for João Rosa and that made him sad. In his stomach the old beast gnawed at him no longer. There was only a quiet, deep, hot pain inside him. Shirt in hand he looked for the nail to hang it on and for a moment his long, thin face was in the light from the door.

'*Ená*, Zeca!?' Grandma had another voice now, curious, more friendly. 'Come over here.'

A smile started and very slowly ideas began to gather in her old head, gathering together the meanings, and she remembered that conversation she had paid no attention to, she had even forgotten it already ... but it's true, Delfina, *nga* Joana's girl, was by the shanty, nearly six o'clock it was, asking about her grandson Zeca and soon as Grandma had sighed that he still wasn't home from work the girl ran off, no thank you or anything, not even an explanation.

'Sit down, Zeca. What's that, why's your eye so red? Did you fight?'

Zeca's hand went up quickly to hide his face but it was too late. Grandma had already had a good look.

27

'Huh! Didn't I tell you, Grandma, the white man *sô* Souto . . .'

'*Sukuama!* The white man *sô* Souto you said was the whip on your back, Zeca.'

'Right, Grandma. On my back. You saw it. But the tail of the whip hit me here; this morning it wasn't hurting, but now in this darkness it seems to be swelling up.'

Grandma Xíxi was standing now. Her thin face, shrivelled and full of lines, was laughing and wrinkling her skin even more, making it hard to tell what was nose and what was lips. Only her eyes, young once again, were shining. 'Ay, child! Seems that all you've got is your bad luck. That whip even caught your eye, Zeca?! When bad luck comes . . .'

In those words Zeca Santos felt Grandma Xíxi was playing with him. He couldn't really swear it but that look, the hurry to get up from the mat, the words not spoken direct; Grandma already knew that Delfina had put that mark on his face. But how, then? Who could have told her? No one else was there. Only if it was that Fina passed by the shanty herself. With that thought – seeing at last the big lie because Fina didn't know Grandma well enough to be talking about such a matter – Zeca's heart grew lighter, beat faster, and his eyes searched Grandma's face carefully to see the proof of his good fortune. But *nga* Xíxi was already down again, busying herself with the day's empty pots and Zeca let himself drift away, enjoying the happiness of thinking Delfina had come by.

Friendly now, Grandma's voice came softly from the empty pots and baskets. 'Look here, Zeca. You like yesterday's fish?'

'Yesterday's fish?! Grandma knows I love yesterday's fish.' His voice was greedy, and without another thought he asked, 'Where is it . . . Grandma?'

His moist tongue caressed his dry lips and he remembered the pieces of charcoaled fish, fat like he loved it, grouper or moon fish it didn't matter, put in the bottom of the pan with its own juices and onion and tomato and *jindungo* and everything else Grandma knew how to cook so well, letting it all sleep covered up until the next day – yesterday's fish – that's when it's eaten.

28

Zeca's eyes searched all over the dark shanty but there was nothing, only Grandma squatting among the empty pots, cans, and baskets.

'Ay, Grandma, where is it? The beast in my belly's hurting me again. Where, Grandma, where's yesterday's fish?'

Standing in front of her grandson, hands on her thin waist, Grandma could not hold back her laughter, her joke. With her finger pointed at him out came the words saved up in her head, 'Listen, child, if you want yesterday's fish, leave money today and you'll find it tomorrow!'

Shocked, his mouth wide open, Zeca looked at Grandma without seeing her anymore. His mouth dried up as the saliva ran to his belly, his blood began to pound in his ears, and the sadness coming from *nga* Xíxi's deceiving words smothered all the joy the thought of Delfina passing by the shanty had put in him. His eye ached. In his stomach the throbbings of his hunger were quiet but his tongue wanted to fill his dry mouth. Miserable, he dragged himself slowly to the door, holding onto the trousers he had taken off to fold up so carefully.

Above the low tin roofs of the *musseque*, overcoming the glare from the searchlamps in their iron towers, a large blue-white moon was climbing in the sky. The little ones were still playing in the wet sand and in the doorways older people were enjoying the freshness, resting a bit from the work of the day. In grassy places crickets were accompanied by frogs in puddles and all the air was trembling with their music. On a branch nearby a *matias* still sang, now and again, his little song asking for five-penny-bread.

A great heaviness took hold of Zeca's heart and the sounds of life from outside only increased the melancholy spreading through his body. He turned back from the door and folded his trousers carefully to save the creases. Then, with nothing left for him to do, he leaned his head down on Grandma Xíxi Hengele's shoulder and began to cry, great sobs like a small boy, long hot tears running down stubborn lines the pains of hunger had left on his face, his child's face.

THE TALE
OF
THE THIEF AND THE
PARROT

A certain Lomelino dos Reis, Dosreis to his friends and ex-Lóló to the girls, was living with his wife and two children in the Sambizanga *musseque*. Better still: in the place where Sambizanga and Lixeira are confused. The people living there insist it's Lixeira for sure. Son of Anica dos Reis, mother, and of a father he didn't know; the closest shopkeeper was Amaral. Or so he said in the police court when he was interrogated. But it could also be one of his lies; they grabbed him holding the sack with seven fat, live ducks and his excuses weren't coming so fast yet.

A friend of his is who saved him. Futa, Xico Futa, bumped into him there in the station house, otherwise Zuzé the assistant would have put the whip to him.

This is how it all started:

He was brought in when it was already half-past midnight, the sack had stayed with the night shift, the ducks moving around inside were cackling like maybe they had figured out their necks had been saved. Zuzé was sleeping at the time and he always got furious when they woke him up just to guard a prisoner. And that's exactly what happened. Full of sleep, his red eyes looking like he'd been smoking *diamba*, he let his hands search the man without paying too much attention, grumbling and calling him names loud enough for him to hear. Dosreis didn't even move; he kept quiet, his arms above his head, but it was in his heart that the fury over that stupid mulatto Garrido was growing, rising, snarling. He'd bet anyone who wanted, he'd swear it, he knew that cripple had squealed on him ...

'Elá! What's this here? Damn, if I stayed asleep ...' Zuzé laughed, his sleepiness had left him soon as he found the little shoemaker's knife in the back pocket. Caught, Dosreis pretended he was rearranging the ragged edges of his torn coat messed up from the search.

'So you're a bandit, huh?'

'I'm no bandit, no sir!'

'Shut up, you are too! You're a bandit ... let's go!'

But Dosreis refused, he didn't like anyone to push him. He had his own legs for walking, not just any *cipaio* was going to shove him around like this, even if it was in the station house it didn't matter. '*Sukua*'! A blade like that can kill some one? You're crazy ... Hey! Don't push! I know the way.'

'Get going! You talking back?'

'Don't push, I just told you! *Cipaios*, think they're so smart.'

And right there in the jail the confusion got worse. Zuzé knocked him down with a blow on his neck and Dosreis jumped up ready to punch him but in the darkness of the cell he got tangled up in the ragged pieces of his coat and the assistant socked him in the face. By that time everyone was already awake with the noise and they began to jeer and yell into the dark, some actually came to separate them, others just insulted their families; what idiots, coming in and interrupting people's sleep, no respect ...

'*Ená!* You good-for-nothing, think you can abuse authorities, do you? I'll give you the whip if you don't get smart, you hear? Can you imagine, such an old man and he still wants to fight!'

'Rags are old! Not me! I'm not afraid of some *cipaio*!' The words hardly left his mouth and he had already butted him, suddenly, so fast no one could believe a thin little body all tangled up in rags could really run like some antelope. Zuzé didn't even have time to get out of the way, he just put his hands out against the man's head when it hit his belly. That's when Futa appeared to separate them and he saved Lomelino just in time.

'*Elá*, Dosreis! Calm down!' He grabbed his arms behind his back, pulling with all that strength he had from lifting full barrels by himself, and Lomelino was in the air kicking his legs and looking like some rag doll. The others wanted to pacify Zuzé, who was furious, so they agreed he was right, no one could just go and butt him right there at his job, he was a policeman and should be respected, and he swore if they let him go he'd give that Cape-Verdian a good whipping.

'Let him be, sô Zuzé. He's drunk, can't you see that?'

'Huh? Drunk? That bandit, I'm going to whip him!'

'That's enough! *Ambul'o kuku*, brother! I know him well, the man's just mad because he's in jail, know what I mean?' Futa's voice was like his body, quiet and big and with the strength that makes others quiet. And they did quieten down. Only now Zuzé wanted Lomelino to take a bath – no one could convince him otherwise, it was ordered on the daily task sheet – every drunk who comes in has to go under the shower to get rid of the craziness ... But already no one was listening, they were just having fun looking slyly at the assistant and talking quietly to Dosreis – there was no justice, a man like him, civilized and clean, sure his clothes were old but that didn't matter, to make him take a bath in the *cacimbo*, at one in the morning, like he was just anyone! – and that was only to make him explode again, insult the *cipaio* so they could have a little more fun.

Meanwhile Xico Futa was accompanying Zuzé to the door, bending way down to talk to him because Zuzé was so short, only about half the size of a cane stalk, and explaining he knew the man and his family and he was a good fellow but it seemed like just at the moment something in him was making him mad. Really, he knew him well, visited him a lot, and could swear he wasn't a troublemaker.

'*Aka!* A good fellow, butting me like that? You don't have to kid me, brother Futa. Today I'll let it go, my friend, only because it's you asking, otherwise ...'

Everything was quietening down again; many had already gone back to sleep. Futa, saying goodbye to the assistant near the bars of the cell, lit his cigarette from the latter's butt. But it really wasn't over yet because the rage inside Dosreis' head was great and he didn't know how to get it out, to find the opening he needed to let in the clean air and warm sun again. All he could remember was that sack of ducks, seven fat little ducks that stayed at the station; he hadn't even got to see them. He'd attacked in the dark, slowly, one by one he put the ducks into the sack, careful not to scare the geese who make so much more noise than all of them that at night it isn't worth stealing them. Remembering all that is what hurt, worse than where the *cipaio* had hit him on the face, above the white hairs of his beard. It had to be Garrido who told on him, it couldn't be anyone else for them to catch him so quick – he hadn't even got to Rangel where he was supposed to leave the sack, the jeep'd found him still near the Widow's *quitanda*. What bad luck! But that stupid mulatto was going to pay, he swore it. And then too there was the other one who had to go hitting him just because he found that little knife.

'*Ximba não usa cuecas!*' he yelled like some *monandengue*.

Some of them jumped up on the benches where they slept to catch him and stop him from getting to the bars. Futa grabbed him under the arms, laughing towards Zuzé to make excuses, putting his finger at his forehead to explain. Then, slowly walking around the large cell while sleep was covering the bodies grouped three by three on each bench, Futa talked to Dosreis like he was the younger one and wanted to hear the wisdom of his elder, but really it was Futa who was doing the advising. Very little light was coming in through the high window and the semi-darkness brought sleep with it. Lomelino was drawing in the hot smoke, and in the quietness of the night only the burning of tobacco mingled with the breathing of the inmates. They sat down on the edge of a wooden bunk, Futa's thick arm protectingly around Dosreis' shoulders like the wing of a hen covering her chick.

'So, *compadre*, you better?'

Lomelino's toothless laugh burst through the darkness and the other had a good laugh too. '*Sukua*', grandpa, you're old but you're still tough.'

'Right! That idiot *cipaio* ...I'd just come in and he didn't wait for anything, he punched me straight away! What was I going to do? Stand there? Damn! Lomelino dos Reis doesn't get beat on without giving it back, brother Futa! And in the face? Not even my mother, may Christ our Lord preserve her!'

35

But now there was fun in his words. Xico Futa watched the 'Francês-1' burning in the old man's uncovered mouth; the cigarette's small and unhurried warmth brought calm and the urge to laugh. Silently the *cacimbo* tried to come in through the window, it was like a tiny little teasing rain.

'You know, brother, the fellow's really not that bad. I know him. But you shouldn't answer him back; he just likes to be in charge, so we let him.'

That's how the assistant Zuzé was, as brother Futa was telling him, explaining all his weaknesses, teaching him, so Dosreis would know how he could get one more piece of bread out of him at breakfast by just asking really nicely, like to an equal person, when Zuzé came in, in the morning, to greet everyone with his rough voice, 'Good morning, gentlemen.'

None of the *uazekele kié-uazeka kiambote* or anything like that, he would only say hello in that other civilized way, but then too he would stay and talk for a while in the good everyday language of his brothers and then Kimbundu could be heard among all the other words; he really preferred it that way because he couldn't speak the good-good Portuguese – only now was he taking the exam to get into the third form – and he refused to speak a Portuguese like all the others did, he just wanted to speak the best Portuguese. And when it was time to start picking the two people, or even four, it made no big difference, to go out with the pails of disinfectant and rags to wash the cells of the white prisoners, well then some good feelings were very necessary to get out of that work.

'Butting with your head, no, brother Dosreis! Just using your head. The fellow's okay. He doesn't use the whip, only when they order him to. And even then he always tries to find some way to get around it. I know him!'

In the narrow window the light was mingling with the *cacimbo* rain. The noise of the sleepers, the heavy smell of many people in a small space, water running in the toilet, not letting a person sleep anymore so he just thinks about what's happened in his life, all this was going on in the dark room. Lomelino's cigarette finally went out but Xico Futa's words of friendship were also warming, helping to cover up the holes in his ragged jacket.

His friend went on to teach him not to refuse to do anything in the mess hall, that work wasn't the same as cleaning the floor, it was better. Then Zuzé would let them stay a long time to wash the dishes and the cement table slowly, they could even whistle and sing, not too loudly, and only later when the work was done would he come with his suit all straightened and tucked in.

'Let it go, brother Lóló. The guy's a kind of boss here. When he inspects, he passes his finger over things, looks in the cups, smells the pans ... but let it go, brother. Don't start after him. Just stay at attention, straight if you can, and whenever he says something, say, "yes, sô Zuzé," or "yes, sôr assistant!"'

And the rest Dosreis saw himself with his own eyes the next day. Zuzé ordered them to come in and all the bread and meat and other food left over from dinner he was saying they could eat or even take to their cell if they wanted. Short and wide, he took out his cigarette case, 'Francês' on one side, filter on the other, and made it easy by choosing with his finger, 'Take from here!'

A cigarette like that felt good, a lot better even than many out of jail smoked with friends and work mates, drinking and talking. It's true you could still call Zuzé a *cipaio* if he wasn't around but in your heart that word didn't mean the same thing anymore.

As they talked night was falling into morning, the light of dawn was beginning to take the shadows away from the room, and the sounds of the new day quietened the silences of prison.

'You sleepy, *compadre*?'

'Nah. My heart's been awake ever since I was hit and even with you praising this friend of yours, my anger still hasn't gone to sleep.'

'And what was it that brought you here? What happened?' His broad flat face was serious, he wanted to keep hold of himself, but it was too much and he burst out laughing, 'Zuzé said they grabbed you with a sack of ducks. That true?'

Only Lomelino dos Reis himself could talk about such a thing, about stealing a bunch of ducks and having the bad luck to be caught by the police, without making it seem that he was some know-nothing petty thief who didn't know his job. So he started straight out with no excuses, talking almost like he didn't care about that idiot Kam'tuta who told on him otherwise no one would ever have caught him; that kind of stealing was work he knew well. 'You remember that fellow, don't you?'

No, no he didn't know him, didn't remember at all this so-called Kam'tuta, Xico responded, thinking maybe it was here that Lomelino's lies were starting.

'*Sukua*'! Skinny, lame boy, always dragging a crippled leg. Mulatto.'

'I don't remember, brother. Crippled? Wait a minute ... Only if it was that one with a shoeshine box right in front of the "Majestic", wait a minute, a light mulatto, his name's Garrido, blue eyes, still only a *monandengue*, right?'

Yes, that's him, Dosreis confirmed; and he explained Kam'tuta was the nickname the kids would call him, you see, brother, the boy's ashamed to sleep with women because of his leg, so ...

Life's crazy: who'd ever guess a clever one like him would also be a stool pigeon who tells on his pals? But at the same time, too, doubt was growing in Futa's head, these tales about petty chicken thieves are always like this: whenever they're caught it's only from someone squealing because they know what they're doing, they never leave a trace for the police, they're masters, etc.

'Look here, Dosreis. Think about it, don't be accusing the boy just like that.'

'Just like that? Me? You know me, brother Xico, you know I'm a man of my word, I don't talk if I'm not certain ... The fellow squealed. Otherwise how would they've found me? How?'

But one thing is what people think, what inside the heart says to the head, already altered by its own reasons, vanity, being too lazy to think more, anger at people, not being too smart; the other thing is the actual facts of a confusion. And this is just what Xico Futa told him. Later, the real facts were well known: at the end of that day's afternoon, Garrido Kam'tuta actually came into the station house, into the same jail as them.

But, before, in the police court, this is what happened:

Lomelino said: Yes, sir, he was Lomelino dos Reis; father, he didn't know; mother, Anica; the same he'd already said to the patrol before they sent him to the station house. He did explain where his home was but he also didn't explain exactly and the police, who were lazy, it wasn't such a big deal stealing seven ducks, didn't pay much attention. They just grabbed him by his old torn coat, the chief even wanted to hit him so he would tell who the others were who helped in the theft. But nothing. Dosreis didn't like telling on his friends and he just went on explaining, mixing up Portuguese words with Creole and Kimbundu, how he had got in there all by himself, yanked the creatures into the sack and so on. Why? Well now, a wife and two children, sô Chief, even with the children working already and his wife washing it wasn't enough, he needed to round out his budget.

'Round out your budget, you idiot?! With someone else's brood?'

'Oh, sô Chief, I don't have my own brood!'

He laughed, happier. Xico Futa had told him the police were going around in really angry moods, one word would make them hit you, but with this case the men were actually enjoying the whole thing, they weren't even giving it that much attention, didn't even want to find out who was going to buy the ducks from him (no one goes out to steal seven beaks just for his own back yard). And that, if they wanted, he would have told, he knew the *Kabulu* had a cousin in the police and they wouldn't bother him much; but this way he would have him good, Lomelino knew all the tricks and when he was feeling lazy and not like doing anything, the *Kabulu*'d have to let him buy some threads on credit.

But police don't ask the questions that would be good for the prisoner. They wrote down the name of who had been robbed – it was Ramalho da Silva – so they could return the ducks, but about who was supposed to get them, nothing. In fact, Dosreis thought it might be better if he brought it up, if he told even though they didn't ask him.

'*Ená, sô* Zuzé! My bad luck, brother Futa! What'd I think like that for? I didn't even say his name, or nothing. Right away they hit me, snarling and telling me to shut up, the police already knew, and if I was protecting myself by being smart I'd get the hippo whip. Finish! Hell, that's when I shut up! When it comes to force, my friends, conversation doesn't go anywhere.'

Zuzé took the opportunity to put in his two cents, the old butt in his belly still hurt in his heart: 'Huh! You mean you didn't go ahead and butt him?'

'Don't make fun of me, sir! Have pity on an old man like me, *sô* Zuzé. Butt a white policeman? You think this is the first time I've been in jail? *Elá!* I've learned a lot.' The last time, he told them, they punched him and even whipped him, but it was a different matter, more complicated, he had to suffer six months too because of the *Kabulu*. That whiteman had his own magic, no one ever caught him, even if his name was given.

'*Ach!* Magic? Shit! May be, but it's his cousin!'

Sure, but even with a cousin in the police they could've grabbed him to pay the fine and nothing like that's ever happened. And besides bad luck even figures in people's business and with the *Kabulu* bad luck doesn't bother to fight. Even the time of his last imprisonment – December of '61, I spent Christmas in jail, may the Lord our God forgive me – over that matter of the barrels of *quimbombo* and a few more of *candingolo*, the wizard got away; he, Lomelino dos Reis, was the one who suffered in jail and that good-for-nothing wouldn't even send him cigarettes or nothing.

'How do you understand such things, *sô* Zuzé? Always every day, at a certain hour, the *Kabulu*'d go there to keep an eye on how the *quimbombo* was doing in the back yard, that same hour they went there, six o'clock without fail, and nothing! Then one day he didn't go and only the police decided to go! How come?'

Sô Zuzé didn't understand either; so he pretended, sticking his finger in the pots, putting on his important face, inspecting the corners of the mess hall looking for some rubbish to yell about, to show off his position.

Lomelino mourned, 'This man just won't let go of me, brother Xico. What'm I going to do? Every time I feel bad I go to church on Sundays with the boys. They understand!'

'Forget it! A person's life is written out and that's it!'

'That month, after the matter of the *quimbombo*, I even looked for work pumping gas and I found it. But the guy went stirring up trouble for me, sneering he'd talk to the boss about me being a thief, tell about my goings-on.'

'Sure, Dosreis! You, with that white skin, they won't know you're Cape-Verdian.'

'And then, that isn't worth anything?'

'It is, brother Dosreis, it is! That way they can say you're the one who's the boss. If it was a black with a lot of barrels, no one would believe it, but this way it's actually good for them ...' Xico Futa talked on, looking for a way to untie his friend's tongue. He felt some words were still missing, things Lomelino didn't want to tell. Because he knew him so well, he didn't like his ways right now, so agitated, angry, like in a rage, a cat backed up to the wall with a dog ready to attack. And now he wasn't even looking people in the face anymore, his eyes always on the floor, seemed like he had a weight over his head, and that wasn't how Xico Futa knew this man always so straight in his talk and in his work, even in his petty thieving or things like that.

But Dosreis wouldn't, couldn't let out what he was hiding, even though a doubt was gnawing inside him now, it'd been growing for some time, since the morning hour when he came back from the police court. He'd like to tell everything, but not with Zuzé there, he was ashamed to put all these things out before the assistant. With Xico Futa, his friend, it was different.

He could talk as an equal, same profession, neighbours, one's hunger was the other's hunger, and only he could really pull out of him that shame growing inside.

'Listen now, Xico.'

Seemed like the wind was shaking his voice and rustling the leaves in his throat, it was trembling so much it was almost disappearing. Now his eyes were the old eyes of Lomelino but full of the water of shame in the midst of the mess hall's darkness. He couldn't stand them like that so he lowered his head again to try to smile. Because this was the truth: it was something that could also be laughed at, he was just thinking about the shocked face of the boy when they would catch him and bring him to the station house to talk about this matter of seven ducks, he wouldn't even know anything about anything, they hadn't let him go because he was a cripple. Garrido would guess the complaint'd come from him, Lomelino dos Reis, the man he called his best friend, the only one who could read and understand even the confessions from his heart hurt so by the girls, his polite way of talking, the brunt of everyone's jokes; he bet he might even cry because he had that sweet *monandengue* heart.

'Why're you laughing, *compadre* Dosreis?'

'It's shame, brother, it's shame!'

His words came slowly, full of sadness, it was hard to confess even when it was a friend who was listening, even a friend from the same line of work, who understands about everything, it was hurting to say that he'd talked about Garrido Kam'tuta there in the interrogation, that yes the boy had helped him that night, he'd been the guard to warn if the patrols came and it all was a big lie because he hadn't even let the mulatto come with him in these activities because he was lame and couldn't jump the fence or run away if there was a fight. But even worse was that the police hadn't even asked him anything, didn't know anything about him, he really felt now he'd been a stool pigeon, no one'd told on him, he'd just bumped into bad luck that night and the patrol'd been suspicious about such a big sack. He'd even gone on to tell more, give his name and everything, Garrido

Fernandes, his shanty was up there, near Rangel, lived all alone just in a corner of some godmother's shanty.

'Oh, let it go, brother! Now, if you go back to the interrogation, just tell them it was all a lie, that it wouldn't help to grab the boy, that he isn't even part of your group or anything like that.'

'Okay. But what if they find him with something at home . . . then what?'

But their conversation had to stop at that point. In the corridor the jailkeeper was shouting his name, angry; quickly he hid the beef sandwich under the rags of his coat and left running, saying his goodbyes over his shoulder.

'Lomelino dos Reis?' The voice came from some ways away, by the door. Already it was two-thirty and the sun was peeking laughingly through the bars, its yellow brightness eating away the ugly darkness of the corridor. Dosreis ran, his rags tangling him up.

'Isn't that idiot with the ducks ever going to get here? Ah, it's you! Faster!'

Faster, faster, Lomelino's heart also was beating and so was the urge to talk in the interrogation room that the accusations he'd made up about Kam'tuta were a lie.

*　　　*　　　*

Xico Futa was saying:

Can people really know, for sure, how something started, where it started, why, what for, who by? Really know what was going on in the heart of the person who starts confusions, looks for them, or undoes or ruins conversations? Or is it impossible to grab on to the beginning of things in life, when you get to that beginning you see after all that that same beginning was also the end of another beginning and then, if you go on like this, backwards and forwards, you see that the thread of life can't be broken, even if it's rotten at some point it always mends itself at another point, it grows, strays, flees, advances, turns, stops, disappears, appears . . . And I'll say this, I know what I'm saying. People talk, the ones who are in the arguments, who suffer through these affairs, these confusions, they tell, and right there, right then, when some confusion happens, each one tells his truth and if they go on talking and disputing, the truth begins to bear fruit, finally it becomes a full basket of truth and a basket of lies because a lie is already a time of truth or its very opposite.

Garrido Kam'tuta came to the station house because he had stolen a parrot. That's the truth. But how can you really know the beginning, the middle, the end of that truth? You can't eat any part of a parrot; you can't sell a parrot because it talks about its owner; a parrot eats a lot of *jinguba* and a lot of corn, a poor little old chicken thief doesn't spend his earnings on such a creature, there's no profit. So why go ahead and steal a bird like that?

The thread of life that shows the why, the how of arguments, even if it's rotten, doesn't break. Pulling it, fixing it, you always find a beginning at some spot, even if this beginning is the end of another beginning. Thoughts, in the heads of people, still have to start somewhere, sometime, from something. You just have to try and find out.

The parrot Jacó, old and sick, was stolen by a lame mulatto, Garrido Fernandes, shy of women because of his crippled leg and nicknamed Kam'tuta. But where does the tale begin? With what he himself told in the station house when he came in and made peace with Lomelino dos Reis who'd made the accusation? With what the assistant Zuzé said, just repeating what he could read on the prisoner's entry notice? With Jacó?

It's just like a cashew tree, a good old tree which gives shade and juicy fruit, whose trunk-thick branches, twisted and bent and intertwined, grow one on top of the other; young ones are born from them and they build a spider's web above the thicker ones where the broad green leaves are set in place, looking like imprisoned flies stirring in the wind. And the red and yellow fruit are bits of hanging sun. People pass by, they don't pay any attention to the tree, they've been seeing it there for years and years, they drink up the freshness of its shade, they eat the ripeness of its fruit, the *monandengues* steal its budding leaves to oil their fishing lines, and no one ever thinks how did this tree begin? Look at it carefully, take off all its leaves: the tree still lives. Anyone who knows says that's where the sun gives it its food, but the tree can live without its leaves. Climb it, break off its young branches, the ones you can see, those are the good ones for sling shots, cut off every one: the tree will go on living with its other big sons of the older trunk–thick branches holding fast to their fat father stuck firmly into the ground. Go mad, call for the tractor or get machetes, cut, saw, break, pull off all the big sons of the father trunk and then go away, satisfied: the tree of cashews is finished, you found its beginning. But the rain will fall and the heat will come, and one morning when you pass by the cashew tree, some shy little green heads are peeping out all over the leftover bit of thickness of the father trunk. And if then with all your rage for not having found its beginning, you come and cut it, tear at it, knock it down, and pull it up by its root, take out all its roots, shake them, destroy them, dry them, even burn them and watch everything flee into the air as black, dark grey, rolling grey, dirty grey, white and ivory bits of smoke, don't start congratulating yourself on the idea that you broke the thread of life, discovered the beginning of the cashew tree ... Go and sit down next to the flame of the fire or at the table made of crate strips in front of the kerosene lamp; let your head, heavy with wine, fall onto the counter at the *quitanda*, or fill your chest with the salt of the sea which comes in on the wind; think just once, for a moment, a tiny bit, about the cashew tree. Then, instead of going on down towards the root in search of the beginning, let your thought run on to the end, to the fruit which is another beginning and there you'll come upon the cashew nut, she's already ripped off her dry dark skin and her green halves are open like a bean and a tiny tree is being born in the earth with kisses from the rain. The thread of life wasn't broken. Moreover, if you want to return again to the depths of the earth on the path of the root, the old cashew nut is going to appear in your head, the hidden mother of the tree of cashews that you knocked down and the buried daughter of another tree. Now your job has to be the same: knock down another cashew tree and another and another ... That's the thread of life. But people who live it can't go on always fleeing backwards, knocking down all the cashew trees; nor can they keep running ahead for very long, causing more cashew trees to be born. A beginning must be chosen: it usually begins, because it's easier, with the root of the tree, with the root of things, with the root of events, of arguments.

So said Xico Futa.

Now then, we can talk about the root of the affair of the arrest of Kam'tuta as being Jacó, the bad-mannered parrot, although further back we're going to meet Inácia, the nice plump girl he loved even though she was short on affection; and ahead Dosreis and João Miguel, people who didn't pay him much attention and laughed at those ideas of a lame boy. The rest comes from what Kam'tuta himself told me; from what Zuzé the assistant talked about when he read the police register; and more from what even I can know about a girl like Inácia and a *musseque* parrot.

In Garrido Fernandes' narrow mouth everything is 'as it so happens'. And people who hear him talk really feel the boy doesn't believe in yes, doesn't believe in no. Once he talked out everything he wanted and it didn't come out any more certain and it was just the same with everything he didn't want; everything was as it so happens.

So, as it so happens, we're going to find him at about five or so on the day before the day when Lomelino was caught carrying the sack with the forbidden ducks, seated in the shade of the *mandioqueira* tree in the Widow's yard, waiting for Inácia. Not that the girl had agreed to a date, not at all, that kind of luck he didn't have yet; but it was right there, with the widowed owner of the *quitanda* of the former *sô* Ruas, that the girl was working. Garrido Fernandes liked to go there late, when the customers were few, to make some conversation, look long at her round body, all the time trying to get up his courage to talk about how he loved her, he wanted to say the pretty things he would be inventing at night in the corner of his godmother's shanty where he was living free. Because everyone knew Garrido liked the girl and it was a joke for all the rest of them who liked to touch the girl in front of him, to invite Inácia to go to bed with them, to make sly digs that hurt him more than her bright taunting eyes, more even than her voice; even when she was scolding him, trying to hurt him, he liked it.

'*Katul'o maku*, you good-for-nothing ...'

She would just say that, Garrido never tried to touch her even with one little finger, she'd play such tricks just to make her friends tease him, call him bold, a lady-killer, party-boy, say the girls couldn't resist his daring hands ... Kam'tuta suffered but not because of the things they'd say, no. Not even because he thought about it hurting, but because of Inácia, they made fun of him like that right in front of her. Why? The idea! There, in the *quitanda*, that's how it usually was with her ignoring him; but at the time of the afternoon's end, when the hot sun is ready to hide and darkness comes with its sly steps, Inácia liked to go and sit down under the *mandioqueira* tree and talk, let him say a lot of things she'd never heard from the others, words that uncovered for her what could never be but would be nice if it could be, to live a life like Garrido promised he'd make for her, even if he killed himself working at some job, it didn't matter. But then, with the sadness of the lie of these words she liked to hear – they were like the warm sweetness of leftover wine – Inácia would start to tease, sneer at his lame leg, his fear of sleeping with women and she'd go on with all those words, ideas, obsessions the madame was teaching her or she was always hearing, and she'd swear, like she wanted to convince herself, she would get married but only to a white man, she wasn't going to go and set the race back by marrying some mulatto, that's for sure.

Garrido would run away, then week after week he'd lurk around, watching, shame-faced, lacking the courage to speak.

His body would become thin, he wouldn't even shave or anything, his eyes, pretty blue eyes from his father, would be covered by an ugly *cacimbo* and, lots of times during his sleepless nights, he'd think it would be better just to kill himself.

But Inácia wasn't spiteful on purpose, she'd guess his suffering and would call him back again. Only the *monandengues*, who never stayed out of anything, kept at him; they'd throw stones at him, insult him, make fun of his crippled leg: 'Oh, Kam'tuta, swing your foot!'

Moreover, it was Inácia who invented this way of taunting him: once in a fit of rage she had yelled this at him and everyone kept repeating it all the time: even the parrot Jacó, who only said bad words in Kimbundu, learned it. And that's what really hurt inside Garrido. From ordinary people he could excuse it; from the *monas* he could duck the stones; from the older boys he would say they had the heart of an alligator or he would keep his mouth shut so there wouldn't be a scuffle, not from fear but no one would accept a fight with him even if he provoked it; and then, with Inácia, he would act just like a donkey, he'd hide his head on his thin chest and put on the face of a little boy who's ready to do something bad.

But our time always comes.

And today Kam'tuta had resolved himself. He got hold of a new courage; all night, all morning, he didn't sleep, just thinking about what he was going to say to Inácia – he would convince her once and for all to live with him, to love him, to lie in his bed, he had to kill this snake rolled around his heart, this lack of air that was covering his eyes, his chest, bewitching his life, not letting him do anything. They had even chased him off his job as guard, he could only think about Inácia, her shining skin would come to him glistening in the middle of the fire's flames, her laughter crackling from the firewood and the thieves had come, they carried five cement sacks, he didn't even hear the noise or anything and his boss had brought him to the station house, he was the one who had to pay for it all.

So there he was in the late afternoon and the only disturbance was with the parrot Jacó, common ordinary creature who was always trying to bite him and let loose a bunch of insults. That battle would go on every day: on one side, sitting on the *massuícas*, Garrido Fernandes, tall, thin because of the nickname his friends and the girls would call him, setting his crippled leg anywhere like it was made of rubber; on the other side, right now hanging from a branch of the *mandioqueira*, the parrot Jacó. Coloured grey, and dirty from all the dust of the years he had behind him, he was a really mean old parrot with only three or four red feathers left in his tail. And they weren't even worth looking at because the creature'd leave his shit drying there. Every day he'd strut around, scratching at his lice, chicken lice, he had a lot of them because he liked to get into the hen house. But Kam'tuta loved that, he loved to see the roosters attacking him, and how all upset the poor thing would have to try and fly out of there even though his wings had been cut.

In this position they were glaring at each other, Garrido's young pretty blue eyes were looking warily out from his thin face; Jacó's little beady yellow eyes through his white-feathered glasses were fixed on the mulatto, watching out for his hands armed with little stones.

Kam'tuta was thinking, he knew a parrot Downtown, and it was quite different; there was even one belonging to some lady that would whistle the national anthem and do the battalion's bugle call and everything. When he thought of that one he even felt sorry for Jacó, snotty and scratching himself, full of bugs.

> 'Golden parrot
> beak of scarlet
> caw ... caw ... caw ... caw...'

The bird would sing this, finishing it off with two whistles, one after the other, to fool the girls, but his yellow eyes were always fixed on the mulatto so he could get away fast from the little stones the boy was getting ready for him. And he'd even scold with that throaty voice every parrot uses for such events.

49

Only he'd improve on it, letting go with more insults in Kimbundu, he even knew how to insult your grandparents.

Distracted as he was, getting his little stones ready, Garrido didn't even notice Inácia who was already there in the doorway, spying on them, enjoying the battle. Purposely she called out to him, 'Kam'tuta!'

That was all Jacó needed! He shat, shaking and flapping his wings, beating on the leaves of the *mandioqueira* like he was accompanying a party band, then he stretched out his neck, so old it was almost bald, and burst out screeching, mixing up whistles and insults and limericks:

> 'Oh Kam'tuta ... tuta ... tuta ... tuuuut...
> Swing your foot ... foot ... foot ... fooooot...'

Garrido's rage at the creature grew and he wanted to grab its neck; he was thinking how wrong it was that a parrot bird should live in a *musseque*, wandering around anywhere, picking up corn and *jingubas* inside the *quitanda*, drinking with the chickens, just walking around on the ground or in the house, not even a perch or a chain or anything, even a pretty cage to sleep in ... But then the wind blew against Inácia's dress, outlining the firm young thighs underneath, and Kam'tuta watched the girl cross the yard, her round body revealing itself in her walk, her full upright breasts not even bouncing: but her white teeth were laughing at him.

'Ah it's you, Garrido! You here already?'

Nothing, not a word of response did he have.

'*Elá!* don't look at me like that. I get embarrassed.'

'Don't tease, Inácia.'

He could sense her large, round, firm rump outlined at the bottom of her dress; Kam'tuta thought how she was always like this, just a piece of cloth over her skin, never even panties ... and it made him shiver, from the top of himself all the way down his crippled leg, but then it fled as he looked at her eyes, quiet and friendly, different from the provocation of her juicy body. Jacó started insulting him again with his chants, but Inácia went to give him some *jingubas*, talking sweetly, like it was actually that creature she loved.

'Now now, my love. That's enough! Here, take this ... you know I love you, hmmmm? My little birdie...'

Garrido couldn't bear to hear these words spoken to the parrot, he swore he felt robbed, a stupid creature was getting her love and he was there getting nothing, it even seemed like Inácia was doing it on purpose. And he said just that, but the girl turned gentle eyes to his blue eyes and asked, 'How can you think such a thing? You, who like me so much?'

'No, Inácia! I didn't mean to say that, I don't think anything. It's just that the creature is so filthy!'

'Filthy? *Sukua'!* Jacó is clean, aren't you, my love, my little parrot?' And on and on she went; the pain grew inside Kam-'tuta's chest, it seemed like she didn't understand how she was wounding him inside, how much it hurt. She even moved her pretty bottom making it shiver, rubbing her face into the parrot's dirty grey one.

'Inácia, listen! Just look at me a minute!'

'Okay, but just for a minute!' She laughed, moving away to take Jacó to the chicken pen, the creature was yelling water, water, mixing that word up with one foul word after another.

Slowly, using the opportunity, Garrido began. Nervously, at first just saying anything that wouldn't give away where he was heading; then, talking about his life as it was without finding work at a real job, just some odd jobs from friends, mending a torn sole, a shoe patch or heel, and, when they would let him, he'd also do some night work, now here he could start saving some coins. Then he twisted his words around to detour, to get on the path he wanted; Inácia already knew how the boy always started out like this, timid, afraid of rejection, but not even five minutes would go by and here would come the conversation he liked, he'd studied Inácia's questions and answers nights and days without stop, he could even fool her, get her to trail along behind him to those conversations that were better for him.

'Listen, Garrido!' if she was calling him Garrido she was

51

already accepting his conversation. 'You really know how to talk, boy, you really do! But if I accepted you, what would people say?'

'Don't pay any attention to people!'

'Huh? They'd say right away ... a cripple, doesn't even work or anything, just steals, how's he going to live and give a wife food?'

'I'll look for work at a real job!'

'You always say that, month after month, and right up to today! And nothing! You don't want to have to pimp for your wife, do you?'

'As it so happens, no, Inácia, don't even think such a thing!'

'But that's how they'd be talking about you! *Sukua'!* That I'd be getting money from other men so you could eat, Garrido. Don't forget about your leg!'

'Oh shit! Leave my leg out of this!'

'See, you're shouting already. Every time I talk the truth with you, you start shouting at me, don't you?'

'Oh don't get mad, Naxinha, I'm sorry! I didn't mean...'

'Naxinha, your mother!'

Her voice sounded annoyed, Kam'tuta could already feel the fear in his chest that she was getting angry.

That's how their conversations always were, too. He was fine when he was only talking about the things he'd dreamed up at night; but later when the conversation came down to real matters, to everyday life, he would pour scorn on Inácia's ideas, saying how she only thought about food, a house, not about love at all, and the end was always the same: she'd be left with the pain of losing Garrido's words, the ones that made her dream, and she didn't want that. So she would hurt him, and if he tried to go on even after she had insulted him, she would get really mean with him so he would get up and leave.

Garrido had sworn, when he came, he would leave with an answer yes or no. If yes, she would sleep with him; if no, he would never talk to her again and he'd try to kill the *quissondes* that were burning in his chest. That's why he didn't give up very fast, he kept his conversation going, but in no way could he get back to the beginning. Inácia was being mean now, provoking, that half-laughing talk coming from her mouth, 'Now look, Garrido!' She was still calling him that, her anger was only just beginning. 'I've already told you once I'm going to be like my madame, you hear?'

The eyes of a beaten dog looked out at her from deep in his face, so carefully shaved and so smooth that he looked like a *monandengue*. And with his eyes like that Inácia got even angrier, they were making her feel the boy was much better than she was, even if he did have those crazy ways of a boy who never slept with a woman, who doesn't know anything about life, thinks you can live on words of love. Because of this she wanted to hurt him, to shame him as she did so often. 'And another thing, Kam'tuta...'

His head fell and his smooth skin wrinkled up, hunger wasn't filling out his skin and sadness aged him even though he was still very young.

'... I'm warning you, eh?! So now you know! When I'm out with my madame don't you even say hello to me, hear? Understand? Don't you dare even say hello! Or else I'll insult you right out there in the street!'

'Okay, Inácia, okay.'

'Shut up, I'm still talking! Or do you think I'm going to wear the dresses my madame is going to give me, put on high heels and lipstick even – if I want to put it on I will, hear? – to be talked to by just some nothing like you? Do you?'

His blue eyes were fixed on her face once again and the beginnings of a smile showed on his small narrow mouth. Didn't this good-for-nothing mulatto have any shame, you insult him and he sits there smiling with a face like I don't know what, he must be crazy. But it was nice, warm, to see such friendship, nothing could end it, even if she slapped him she bet he'd come back one day. Then she felt ashamed of the words she had said to him, but she still didn't want to ask his pardon because then the boy would think he'd convinced her. But she couldn't hide all her thoughts, there was a great brightness in her eyes, they grew wide in her pretty broad face, her skin taut across it, seemed like they were going to fill it, fill everything, with that light they were giving off.

'Okay, Inácia, I'm sorry...'

Garrido risked this with the permission from her eyes. Inácia didn't respond, she just looked at him, there was confusion in her head, she didn't know anymore how to deal with this different man, he didn't get cross, he was so defenceless you could go on insulting him and everything, but there was a little strength in his words, maybe if people did what he wanted, maybe it would turn out all right, who knows? But how could she go now and live with a cripple, the whole *musseque* around there would know, him with his shame about his leg, he had never slept with a woman, people would make fun, a girl like her, Inácia Domingas, so pretty and smooth and firm, to take up with a man like him with so many others around who wanted her? And even worse, he had no work or boss.

The afternoon was fading quickly because it was the time of *cacimbo*, the day was fleeing early from the cold, from the wind rustling in the leaves. In the yard Jacó was screeching insults, whistling and chanting while he hopped around to keep away from the pecking of the roosters. Inácia was quiet, sad, she scratched at her big toe, letting her head run with Garrido's words.

'You got a *bitacaia* there, Inácia?'

'Huh? *Sukua'*! You think I live in a rubbish dump?'

But she was laughing as she bent over her foot, scratching it with her fingernail, she felt like playing again. She stuck her leg out in front of him, saying, 'Yes, Garrido, I really do. Would you believe it, where in the world did I get it?'

'There's chickens here, dirt in the yard...'

'Can you get it out for me? Huh? If you like me it shouldn't be hard, should it?'

That was just like the Inácia he loved to watch, without getting into it himself, the girl they would try to touch in the *quitanda* and she would always get away and laugh and make fun and play with them all. Only with Garrido, no, he didn't even want her to, nor did Inácia have the courage to let him but then, to get even, she'd make fun of him.

'Okay. Get me a pin.'

'*Elá!* Get closer! You're not going to get it out from way over there.'

He moved up next to her and it seemed like the cold *cacimbo* wind had suddenly become hot.

'Sit down on the ground, Gágá, it's easier.' Her voice held sweetness again and her eyes were soft. Slowly, like a cat, she stretched her foot out against his stomach, the broad bare foot of a *musseque* girl, right above the middle of his legs to tickle him, and a burning match ran through Garrido's blood, hot pepper, *quissondes* biting him, it felt good. So the confusion in him would go away he began to peck with the pin but he was all thumbs, the point wouldn't stay still, he couldn't get at the flea's head. It was a young *bitacaia*, had only just started to work its way in, half in, half out, it looked like it was peeking out, spying on them, to tease them, it hadn't even made its egg sack yet. That's why it caused so much itching. And in these matters Kam'tuta's technique was to press a fine needle flat against the skin and advance slowly, pierce its body just a tiny little bit and then – bam! – yank it out. But how was he going to do this now when he was shivering all over with chills from the heat of his blood and Inácia's warm arm around his neck to keep her from falling over and her soft firm breasts, her ripe body smell, were touching him, he could feel it through all the holes in his clothes? Flustered he raised his head a bit to take a deep breath, to see if the heat would go away, but that was the worst thing he could have done, his head actually fell back down with the weight of the blood pounding all through him, the beating of a party drum in his ears.

Inácia had pulled her skirt up above her smooth round knees and Garrido felt a burning in his eyes, shutting out everything else, that shining black skin glistening there in the darkness between her long firm thighs and the feeling wanted to pull his head up a little further to sneak another look and another, that paleness was so nice calling him from there down at the end of the full darkness of her body, Garrido could swear there wasn't another colour prettier than that one, a clean clean paleness there in the depths of the night of her skirt, darker now with the real night that was coming fast, maybe just to cover the redness of Garrido Fernandes' face.

'*Ená*, Gágá, stop shivering! Hold on with your other hand.'

He took hold of her nicely shaped ankle, squeezing it tenderly. Seemed like heat was running over his arms like rain water, leaving his body hurriedly to go into Inácia's leg, she'd bent down even lower like she wanted to watch the work more closely but, as she breathed, her soft breasts were caressing Garrido's *monandengue* head. Maybe, who knows, the *bitacaia* was by now making fun of Kam'tuta's failure, he, who was the master over those *mauindos*, could not get hold of it. It was true the pin was thick but someone like him should be able to work with any kind of tool.

He felt the *bitacaia* could just move in, lay its eggs, make its *mauindo*, at this point he didn't even care; if he could go on like this with the *quissondes* attacking his blood more and more and that tease Inácia moving closer, leaning on him, showing him the secrets of her body, provoking him like this, he might even think maybe she wanted him, maybe he should grab her right there, behind the hen house, because the night would help now, darkness was coming.

But what did come, in a crooked swoop, was *Jacó*. He landed on his mistress and started pecking at Garrido, ruining what he was trying to do, chasing him all the way to the *mandioqueira* tree.

I said the root of this tale was Jacó and that's the real truth, because if it wasn't for that creature getting all of Inácia's affection, nothing would have happened, Kam'tuta would never have agreed to what the girl asked him at the end, and it was shameful, he wasn't a *monandengue* any more to be going around doing such a stunt.

But how could Garrido stand it, wanting Inácia so much, wanting her to be his girl, to stop the ache in his heart and kill the *quissondes* that ran through his blood, what was he going to do if a filthy, old, bad-mannered parrot could go and put a kiss on the girl's mouth and hide beneath her legs?

Night was coming but it had already entered Garrido's heart the moment Inácia decided to end up infuriating the boy with Jacó. She whispered so you could hardly hear her, 'Kam'tuta, swing ...' She didn't even have to finish it. Straight away Jacó opened his wings, made a noise like a real person laughing, but instead of talking he sang,

> 'Kam'tuta ... tuta ... tuta ...
> Swing your foot ... foot ... foot ...'

And then Inácia went on piercing his heart. 'Move!'

Jacó didn't wait. Louder than ever he sang,

> 'Swing your foot ... move it ... move it ... move it ...
> Swing your foot ... foot ...'

And she even thought up something else, to finish off the game, she took a nut out of her pocket, put it in her mouth and said, 'Jacó, Jacó get the little nut!'

Jacó came and with his chuckling song pecked her on the mouth and took the *jinguba*. For Garrido it was like being punched every time the parrot did this. He couldn't stand it anymore. 'Inácia! Make fun of me if you want. But don't let that bastard fool around your mouth, Filthy creature!'

With the face of an innocent little girl she fixed her large eyes on Garrido's face. 'Oh? Is that bad?'

'Yes, Naxa.'

She didn't even scold him for calling her that name she hated. 'Okay, I'm jealous of that thing! Now you know!'

At that moment there wasn't another face in the world as cunning as Inácia's. 'You don't say? You're mad because the parrot gave me a kiss like that?'

'As it so happens yes I am, Inácia. Don't do it anymore!'

'And if I say to him: "Jacó! Look for the nut..."'

Then, all he had to see was the parrot sticking his beak, his whole head into her large cleavage, trying to get at the *jinguba* Inácia had put there between her heavy breasts which trembled with the flapping of the bird's wings. Garrido couldn't even tell any more what he was feeling: whether it was the *quissondes* or the hot pepper running through his blood, thinking about Jacó pecking slowly around her breasts in that way; whether it was the fury of wanting to wring the neck of that vulgar creature that could move around where he was even ashamed just to look.

'You also jealous of my breasts, Gágá?'

'Yes! As it so happens, I am! And I hate Jacó!'

'And if I let him walk under my dress, are you going to get mad, Gágá?'

'As it so happens, I am! As it so happens I could even strangle him. I swear it! Inácia, don't do that, don't, don't provoke me like this, Naxa!'

But now Jacó's head came up from the breasts to swallow the nut he'd found, and Inácia laughed all over, twisting and turning from the tickling of his feathers.

'Keep still, Jacó! You're making me ticklish!'

'It's the son-of-a-bitch's fleas!'

'Jacó doesn't have fleas! You've got fleas! Jacó ... Jacó ... it's going to rain!'

With these words came the last straw, no one could have gone on being taunted like that in such a degrading way. The parrot slowly got down and was poking his head between Inácia's closed knees. He went in under her hem and started to walk around in there, into the darkness, letting out calls and whistles, and crooning, 'The rain is coming ... the rain is coming...'

Squirming with the tickles, Inácia laughed at Garrido Fernandes' furious face. And when the boy slowly got up and started dragging himself away with his crippled leg, humiliated, wretched and ashamed, Inácia called to him gently with her voice full of brown sugar, 'Gágá! Don't leave me alone in the dark.'

58

Darkness really had come, lights were beginning to twinkle everywhere, and in the *quitanda* you could already hear the sounds of men spending money on wine on their way home from work. Garrido stood still, confused, not knowing whether to leave or to stay; maybe she was calling him just so she could keep making fun of him, her voice was lying, she didn't mean to use Gágá. But, slowly, he came back to sit down next to her and pleaded, 'First, if you want me to stay, get rid of that son-of-a-bitch Jacó!'

Inácia agreed and shoved the parrot away from her; the creature fell onto the ground, heavy and lopsided like some fat squat duck, calling out the insults that *sô* Ruas had taught him and he had never forgotten.

'Then, if you want me to stay and take care of you until your madame gets here, let me give you a kiss, too.'

'*Elá*, you shameless . . .'

Kam'tuta himself had no idea how those words came out of his mouth, he hadn't even thought of them before then, maybe the heat in his blood was giving him the courage to say such a thing. Inácia laughed hard, putting music in Kam'tuta's ears, and her coconut teeth were shining in the dark. 'Okay! I agree!'

Flustered, not expecting her to say yes, Garrido raised his arms, but his head was working faster than his hands and he felt, even without touching it, the warm skin of her back that he was about to embrace, the soft down of her broad lips, the warm moisture of her mouth, everything was just like in his dreams as he lay wide awake in the darkness of the corner where he slept and made up events that would never ever happen.

'Wait a minute! You can give me a kiss and if you want I'll even let you put your hand on my leg. But I get something in return.'

'Anything, anything! I'll do it!'

'You swear?'

'On my mother's soul!'

'Okay then . . . I heard that you can actually walk upside down

59

'... so put your hands on the ground, put your bad leg around your neck and walk around the yard so I can see you!'

'No!' A heavy pain, a longing to strike out, came into his hands raised to embrace her. 'No, Naxa! Don't make fun of me like that!'

'Huh? Make fun? How? Just to show me...'

'No! I'm not a clown! And even if I can do that, it's not just a stunt! It's because I'm crippled and Our Lord God made it that way!'

'Okay, forget it! It's your decision, Gágá. If you don't want to kiss me, if you don't like my legs, that's up to you. But then don't go saying I'm stingy with you, that I only like the others!'

He wanted to cry, to shout, to tear at that innocent little-girl face of Inácia's looking at him quietly with her big eyes afire. But his hands refused to hit her, all they wanted was to embrace her, hold her tightly against his narrow, starved, thirsting body. With tears which were close to raining down, he lowered his head, spread his thin arms and put his long hands on the ground. He didn't even need to catch his balance or anything, his body just hung there upside down, one leg in the air and the other skinny and shapeless, immediately wrapped itself around his neck.

Silently he straightened up his *monandengue* head. He looked at Inácia sitting there, and he saw the sadness, the pity, coming on her already, seeing him in this position it was like he was only half a man. But he couldn't look at her any more, he started walking. Each step with his hands down drove a thorn into his heart, a weight that grew, that wouldn't let him move faster, but he wanted to finish quickly, quickly, to flee from that figure that he himself could see going rapidly around the yard, almost racing now, to kill the shame, so no one could see, to win the prize, to run away, far away.

'Okay, Naxa, I've done it.'

His voice was so sad, so sad. His blue eyes clouded over. There was no strength left in his arms to hold her. But the *quissonde* returned to sting in his blood, seeing Inácia so quiet like that defeated, not moving at all, only her eyes staring out from under the *mandioqueira* tree, not the same person now, she looked just like a little girl. A great tenderness overcame all of Kam'tuta's shame, put out the sadness, forgave Inácia's mischief, wanted to caress her, to say sweet things to promise and fulfil, but now all he could do was get down, smiling, for a better embrace than he'd wanted at first, without the hot pepper in his body, not needing to press her against him, but to lean her against him, just to play with her hair, to stroke the skin of her round shoulders, to repeat softly in her ears those words he knew she liked to hear.

And if he hadn't been thinking like this, if he hadn't been full of that happiness that always comes when you think nice things about someone, he would've fought, he would've beaten Inácia, it didn't matter if she was a woman, she had no right to make fun of a man like that. But no, happiness wouldn't let him. Inácia's slap, the girl's screams in the midst of her tears, her lying laughter, just shocked him even more, open-mouthed, the slap on his face didn't even hurt him, his big deep blue eyes stared at her astonished, everything seemed to be happening through the smoke of *diamba*, Inácia screaming crazily, insulting him as she ran into the *quitanda*, 'You good-for-nothing mulatto son-of-a-bitch! Lame legless shit! Think you can buy me with some monkey trick like that? Get moving. Out! Get out of here, you mulatto ape, you buffoon!'

Slowly, dragging his crippled leg behind him, his heart broken, his blood cold, colder than the *cacimbo* of his tears and the night closing over the *musseque*, Garrido could feel for a long time Jacó's whistles, the taunting voice of that son-of-a-bitch parrot, sneering at him from inside the *mandioqueira* tree, 'Kam'tuta ... swing your foot ... your foot ... foot ... foot ...'

*   *   *

João Miguel, the one they called Speedy, was the leader. No one disputed that, it was fact to all of them, nor would they

61

think it could be any other way. But the man they trusted was the Cape-Verdian Lomelino dos Reis because only he could talk to the *Kabulu*, without that man their business would go nowhere. And with Garrido Fernandes, Kam'tuta, they were a gang. A gang by accident really, no one had ever organized them or anything, and it only got going like that from their need to be together because they drank together and their houses were close to each other. One day, without even having planned it, they broke into the showcase of a barber's shop and realized that it was Lomelino who had done the job, Speedy who had helped and Kam'tuta who had stayed behind pretending he was peeing on the wall while watching out for the patrols. Okay, so it stayed that way: the leader was João Miguel, he was the one who split up the money; it was Dosreis who got it by selling the perfume and other things to the *Kabulu* and they all kept on trusting him otherwise they couldn't go on with their work; Kam'tuta, crippled like he was, was only good for being a look-out. He would stay on watch, but sometimes so as not to upset him the others wouldn't even tell him about a job if they were going to have to run for it. In the end they would give him his share: half of a half if he didn't go with them; an equal share if he did go. That way he could never tell on them.

They always met here in Amaral's *quitanda*, eight-thirty, time when they started leaving the shanties, with dinner already in their bellies, after spending the day around the Downtown look-ing for real work, or after sleeping in the yard when it was the day after some job. João Miguel was always the first to arrive and when Dosreis came in the boy had already drunk more than half a litre with soda the way he liked it. But on that night of the ducks everything that started, started happening backwards, just like it had guessed it was going to end up differently, that something was going to happen.

When Lomelino arrived, tired from the walk from Rangel and beyond, João Miguel hadn't yet appeared. He asked the employee Luís but he said no, Speedy hadn't been there. It was almost nine o'clock, maybe the boy had gone to the pictures with a girl, but when that happened he always let them know first. But today he had to come, he had left him a note with his neighbour Mariquinha to meet him at Amaral's at eight-thirty. Okay, so he'd wait.

Sitting in their corner, Lomelino lit a cigarette, but his mind wouldn't stay calm, he couldn't handle this waiting even for a friend, though it still wasn't that late yet. No. His thoughts refused to accept this and little by little the passing of the minutes filled him with worry. It would be a shame if they lost this good dark night to take care of their duck business at Ramalho da Silva's, over there in the Marçal *musseque*. He had already been studying it for quite a while, ever since João Miguel found out how easy it would be to pull it off and with a sure profit. But with a sure profit only if Lomelino helped with those contacts of his. It was hard to convince the *Kabulu*, the man didn't appreciate this business of handling stock, he just wanted things he could hide in an empty shanty without anyone noticing, with creatures that move around and make a noise you have more work to do and the police always find them. Dosreis told him the quiet goods were being well guarded now and there were too many patrols and furthermore in these times getting into a strange house is dangerous, people shoot too fast and then give the excuse that it was a terrorist and that's it, end of discussion. So, about seven o'clock that day, he went back there to get an answer, propped up on the counter, acting like he was only there to drink his half-litre. *Sô Kabulu*, fat and red, came over to him but all he said was, 'Bring them to Zeca Burro's house!'

Great! He knew Zeca Burro well, he slaughtered stolen goats to sell their meat, they'd even done some business with him once over some she-goats that were getting old and sick and it had brought a profit. With him it was a cinch; but the worst thing was that it was the *Kabulu* who had talked to Zeca Burro about this affair and it was that scrooge who would take the profits, he bet he'd only pay them less than half of what the Kinaxixi market'd bring for beaks and then would get more than double from Zeca Burro. And they were some good fat ducks, they didn't grow up on rubbish, waddling around the *musseques*, that's for sure. There was even one, almost all white, that he had seen close up, that might even burst if it got any fatter, he bet it was four kilos already.

He left the *Kabulu*'s shop right away, went through the darkness at a slow pace to gain time and not get too tired, his breathing had started playing tricks on him, during these days of work his heart would beat faster and his blood, accustomed to the laziness of quiet work, started flowing fast with the thought of the darkness, the job, and also that maybe João Miguel would scold him for his having forgotten all about Zeca Burro because now they were going to lose a good profit from those fat ducks. But João Miguel would understand, the boy was really still only a *monandengue*, only twenty-four years old, he would obey him like a father, with that respect for an elder. Unless the boy had been dreaming again about the past and was high from *diamba*. Maybe that's why he wasn't there at the agreed time, just because he'd gone smoking. And all alone, too, not even Kam'tuta at least was with him. But that one, he knew the boy was always around the Widow's *quitanda* these days to see Inácia, he looked like a rooster with that big head on top of his skinny neck and dragging his leg along, may Our Lord God forgive him, he shouldn't be making fun of a cripple, but Kam'tuta really did look just like a rooster.

'Good evening, *compadre* Dosreis!'

It was Speedy and he sat down fast like his body was too heavy for him. He sat there staring thoughtfully at Lomelino's face as if he'd never seen it before in his life, his eyes almost closed, quiet, all bloodshot, breathing slowly but heavily like the gusts of steam from a train engine. Whenever he saw him like this Dosreis would think the boy really was a steam engine. It wasn't just because his job was as a railway switchman when he was working for the C.F.B. in Luso, nor because of the tales he told about the things that happened to him on the railway. But those eyes of his, quiet like that and red, they looked just like the lights of a locomotive. The force of the wind of his breathing from his mouth would come out with cigarette smoke and his broad nose, flat like the front of the train engine, would whistle at the same time. Husky and all scrunched down in the chair with only his head stuck up above the table, he looked like he was making a huge effort to haul a bunch of freight cars full of ore. But the truth was that João Miguel had just finished smoking *diamba*. And he didn't feel like talking.

'How're you doing, João?'

'Okay, thanks, brother Dosreis.'

Silence again. It was hard to get a conversation going with him like this, you had to leave him alone a little longer, let the plant's venom melt into his blood with the speed with which he walked and come out again through his breathing. It could even be dangerous to talk, even though João Miguel usually only got sad because he didn't want to smoke any more, he would only smoke when the past would really begin to threaten him and keep him from sleeping.

'How about a glass, João?'

'Okay, thanks.'

The warmth felt good inside him, he felt peaceful, and had no desire to do anything at all, except smile and smile, think good things, sing. But the past wouldn't leave him alone, it was deep, very deep, because Félix had been a good friend and the magic of *diamba* couldn't reach that far down. Even if he could take out the root he wouldn't be able to blot out the blood spread over the rails, the wheels of the engine, nor that picture of Félix, completely destroyed, his head on the other side of the stones between the rails, and his body, the body of just a child, all twisted up, and the way his legs, with the weight of the wheel on his neck, had lifted up, it looked like he had put them in the air like when he did exercises at the club, it even made you want to laugh. No, nothing could take that blood from the depth of his eyes, the body of Félix dead like that, killed by him, him, João Miguel. He remembered clearly, the 205, carrying its load of wood to fuel the other trains, was approaching slowly; Chaveco, the engine driver, waved to him and Félix was making faces, his arm around the driver, teasing João and warning him with laughter, 'Later on, at five! Practice!'

And it seemed he really could still see the laughter of the men in the darkness of the cab, the white smoke surrounding them like a big fog, feel forever that laughter in his ears. And then? ...

'Brother Dosreis, this wine is shitty!'

'It's the same as all the rest, João.'

'But it's shit!'

'Okay, I know what you're going to say.'

'That's right! That's just what I'm thinking: a good full glass of our home-made corn liquor, you drink that, sit down on the ground with your friends, talk 'bout life, 'bout work, 'bout girls, the *mutopa* nice and full ... *Aiuê!* I miss it, brother! The full *mutopa*, good tobacco, the water gurgling in the gourd, puff, puff ... Not this filthy *diamba*, not this shit the whites call wine ...'

And the long silence again, only the cigarettes burning and the blood and the voices of the foremen running, the boss, the telegraph lineman, the agent, the assistant cashier, all of them punching him, black bastard and other things, drunk, bandit ... But who cared about Félix more than him, who? Sure, but it was his hand, his, João Miguel's, that sent the 205 against the ore train; it was his hand that put the wheel of the 205 over Félix's neck, such a weak child he couldn't handle the shock of the collision, he fell down there below and the engine, in a small lurch forward, stopped right on his neck.

'No! I can't take this anymore! I can't, brother Dosreis, I can't ...'

'Calm down! Look, let's go outside right now, I need to talk to you, it's serious, we've got a job ...'

The cold *cacimbo* wind was chasing pieces of paper in great gusts all around the *musseque*. In the distance the street lights seemed to have become liquid, their foam falling to the ground or rising in the air like smoke from a fire which has no green wood on it and is burning well.

'Did you set it up?'

'Yes. The same one. He said yes, we can deliver 'em. But it's further away, he doesn't want them at his place. That the fellow'll wait till midnight. It's Zeca, I don't know if you know him...'

'Zeca Burro?'

'That's him.'

'Isn't that fellow a friend of yours?'

'No, not at all, I don't even know him to say hello to,' lied Dosreis. 'And the rest is up to us.'

'Okay, let's make plans.'

The air felt fresher and the conversation was making Speedy better. He was talking straighter, he still had those big eyes wide open but in his head everything was working fine, all the whys and wherefores he took care of immediately, besides he knew that yard like the back of his hand and the layout was easy, the house lay right at the back of some shanties, only a narrow little alley led up to it and the patrols didn't pass very close to it.

'What time?'

'Eleven-thirty's good. We'll finish it fast and then you can go off and mix with the people who'll be leaving the pictures.'

Dosreis, anxious, was saving up that special question for the very end. During these days of *diamba*, no one knew why, but João didn't like Garrido any more; those two who every day would be arm in arm in their various conversations about people and about the ways of living life, it was really something. But now it was also true that whenever Speedy thought about Félix he didn't want Garrido's friendship and they barely escaped fighting.

'João, are we going to take Kam'tuta?' He had scarcely put the question before the boy's no came loud, in a shout, it was plain he wasn't going to have it any other way.

'But look... He could stand at the top of the alley and whistle when the patrols...'

'No! We don't need him! I'll do the job; you stand watch. Then you take them in the sack and that's that. I don't want a cripple dragging along on my legs!'

'Okay, okay, don't get cross. Anyway we haven't always taken him along on other jobs and the boy understands.'

'No! I don't want that crippled shit, I just told you! I'm not even sure he isn't a stoolie, with those conversations of his 'bout changing his life to start living with...'

'*Elá*, Speed! What're you talking about? How can you accuse him like that? I've known him since he was a kid, João, and you're his friend, too.'

'Friend! me? I only like whole people, I don't go around with half-men ...'

'I didn't think you talked about people behind their backs, my friends!'

João hadn't finished talking when that voice jumped out of the darkness, he'd been standing there, and it froze Lomelino's soft heart, seemed like all his blood fled with shame at that moment. But not in João Miguel's breast: his rage only grew, giving fire to his urge to strike out, to tear at himself, to pound at his own body.

Dragging his leg which always seemed like it was going to be left behind, Garrido moved out from the darkness at the edge of the *quitanda* and came over, slowly, his eyes and his head held high. Dosreis moved towards him; João Miguel backed away against the wall.

'Now listen, Garrido! I can explain ...'

'Never mind, friend Dosreis. I heard everything. When I got here you were talking about when to start the job and I stood there listening ...'

João Miguel jumped out, furious. 'Didn't I tell you? Didn't I? You're nothing but a stoolie!'

Dosreis held him back, stood in the middle, his old body between them.

'Just don't be insulting me, João! As it so happens I'm your friend, but I'm not going to let them make fun of me any more. I swore that!' And the boy's blue eyes showed a new strength, Lomelino had never seen them like that. Even his leg seemed all right, coming out straight from his shorts. Garrido was standing

68

completely upright, his thin body erect, but the most amazing thing was the calmness on that *monandengue* face, his eyes straight on João Miguel so he could barely stand it, he had to lower his big steam-engine head and Kam'tuta said again, one word at a time, 'Everyone makes fun of me, but no more, brother Dosreis! And even you, João Miguel, my friend! You're the one I'm going to warn first, you worked yourself up against me, I didn't do anything to you. Whenever I go on the jobs, I do just what you do. You don't have anything to blame me for. When you came you found me with my *compadre* Dosreis. Why should I have to be left out now? Because I'm crippled, lame, half-a-man like you said? No one is going to make fun of me any more. I'll fight, I swear I'll fight! I don't even care if you beat me to death, do you hear? Do you hear me, João Miguel?'

The boy really seemed to be crazed. He pushed Dosreis out of the way; Dosreis let him by, shocked by this new straightened-up Garrido. But now he wasn't too afraid, nothing was going to happen, João would never actually fight Kam'tuta.

'Listen to me! As it so happens you're my friend so I'm warning you, okay? I'm not afraid, keep that in mind. Not of you, not of any bastard in this whole *musseque. Sukua'!* Crippled, half-a-man! Look: you're big but you're no good for anything; your body's grown but your heart's still little, twisted, full of rubbish.'

'Shut up, Garrido! Shut up or else . . .'

'Hit me, if you can! Go ahead! That's just what I want you to do, can't you see that? I want to fight! At least fight with a man for once, with someone who isn't afraid. Go ahead, hit me, if you've got the guts!'

There in the night Garrido Kam'tuta grew straight, no longer the lopsided boy with his head always down, hiding in every corner, running from the *monas* who chased after him with insults – 'Kam'tuta, swing your foot! Swing your foot!'

And João Miguel saw Félix rising again in front of him. It was still his friend talking to him there, being reborn in Kam'tuta

with those brave words he always had ready, that way of his
of seeming to win even when he was getting a real beating. He
clenched his big hands, hiding them in his pockets, they wanted
to come out on their own and attack Garrido if he wasn't going
to shut up, he couldn't hear any more, he couldn't let in any
more of those words he was saying and that were ruining all
the good patient work of the *diamba*. He couldn't go on feeling
the truth like that burning in his ears, inside his head, outside
his head, he'd better run away or he would smash that mulatto,
him with his weak body.

'Shut Garrido up, Dosreis, shut him up or I'll kill him!'

'You're a coward, João! You're afraid of the truth! You've
got nothing in your heart but a nest of scared rats. Accept what
happened, get over the guilt you carry around. Don't be so
scared, don't hide in *diamba*, fight with the pain, fight with life,
don't hide, you big chicken, all you know how to do is beat
up other people, weaker ones, but with yourself you don't know
how to fight, you're scared. You're rotten! I'm ashamed to be
your friend any more!'

Lomelino ran to grab him but he missed. The mulatto moved
like he was bewitched, even with that leg he ran like it wasn't
even crippled any more and he butted João Miguel straight in
the belly.

'Let 'm go, João! The boy's drunk!'

But João Miguel wouldn't listen, not even the ever-wise
words of his friend Dosreis mattered any more, now the rage
was in his hands twisting inside his pockets, he thought about
strangling the mulatto, that skinny bony neck had just the right
shape for his hands. But a *cacimbo* rain was rising in his heart,
he felt it reaching the windows of his eyes; those words that
no one had ever dared to say to him were gnawing in his ears,
echoing in every corner of his body; and his heavy head was
bursting like its bones were too small to hold in everything that
he was thinking, everything that Kam'tuta's words had let loose
inside there, now no one could tie them down again.

He moved towards Garrido; with just one hand he shoved

Dosreis who fell against the wall; then he stopped smack in front of the mulatto, all you could hear was his frightened breathing. The head butt was nothing, but those deep blue eyes in a child's face, those he couldn't accept, he couldn't allow them to sneer in his face like that, they couldn't go on saying everything silently like that. He raised one huge fist, like the heavy piston rod of a locomotive, over Kam'tuta to smash it down on his head.

'Go ahead!' Garrido said calmly.

Nothing. Only the silence of the wind somersaulting around the shanties.

'Go ahead, coward!' Kam'tuta repeated.

Like the branch of an *imbondeiro* tree his huge arm was lifted in the air, and Lomelino prayed inwardly, there was nothing more he could do now, that João wouldn't let it fall, it would kill Garrido.

'Go ahead if you've got the guts!'

Garrido's voice was trembling now, but his eyes were still the same, fixed on João Miguel's face, he couldn't get away from their light, he was stuck there, imprisoned by that new courage of a weak man, he no longer needed a big body to challenge him like that, to show how a person can stand up to what life does when he has to.

'Let the boy go, Speed! Please!'

It was like being punched for João to hear Dosreis' voice like that, pleading, it hurt more than everything else, an elder like him didn't have to plead, he ordered. Shame came quickly, all his blood drained away; it was Lomelino's slightly hoarse voice that lowered his arm, his eyes, all of João's large body. In a rage and longing to strike out but this time at Lomelino, not knowing now what to do anymore, João Miguel started to run away over the dirt towards the cold and the lights melting into the *cacimbo*, with Lomelino dos Reis not far behind.

Slowly Garrido Kam'tuta turned around in the darkness, once again dragging his crippled leg behind him. All of his courage had fled with his friends and now he just went to lean against the wall of the *quitanda*, all of his strength gone. Then he sat down on the ground and began to cry, silently.

*   *   *

At the same time the patrol came upon the Cape-Verdian Lomelino dos Reis and grabbed him with a sack full of fat ducks, Garrido Fernandes Kam'tuta was stealing the parrot Jacó.

But first he suffered a lot, more than all the other days when he would lie down in his room and just think all night long about things life didn't want to give him because of this bad luck of his to have a leg crippled from paralysis when he was a child. More – the other times there wasn't that much confusion, everything happened in one straight line, he could sense strongly what it was that was making him suffer, what was making him happy, and like that it was easy to decide, his eyes wide open in the darkness, that if he got a real job it wouldn't be hard to resolve the other matter of a woman to live with him. Even when he would imagine some things that were too good, like a wedding, this his friend João Miguel doubted, saying – yes, women are nice, a man can't live without a woman to caress him, to help him, to bring up the *monas*, to cheer him out of sadness, to share his happiness, even his work; but also, and this is what Kam'tuta didn't want to believe and so Speedy would say he was a *monandengue* who didn't know about life, women are the root of our suffering; women talk too much; marriage isn't just laughter and the warmth of lying down at night to rest from the day's work, it's not just the happiness of having someone look straight into your eyes and you trust her. Life is very complicated, dreaming only sets you back or puts you ahead when you let these same complications into your dream along with the good things, and this a boy like Garrido Fernandes couldn't understand yet, not that he was stupid, but simply because he had lived so little his head could only understand the good things that he would invent.

Even such conversations didn't hurt him on those nights when he thought about them; if he felt pain it would only be from Inácia's tricks, from the shame of his leg, of wanting to live with the girl, and of his need for a good job to change his life. But tonight was very different from all the others: before there wasn't rage in his thoughts, there wasn't vengeance; everything that he thought could be resolved as it so happens, he had just left alone. Now it was past ten and the sobs would not leave him, his heart was tight, so many things had happened. That last trick of Inácia's of taunting him with the parrot Jacó left an open wound inside him, in fact the moment came when he thought the best thing would be to kill himself, was it worth going on living as the brunt of everyone's jokes? Then his hatred of himself passed to Inácia, he imagined his hands grabbing her soft black neck, squeezing and squeezing, he would look her straight in the eye, watch her get pale, die little by little, the flame in her eyes going out, going out slowly until they were dark. But thinking like this he had almost started to cry again, he knew that afterwards he would go and mourn for her in the graveyard, he would bring flowers to her grave every Sunday, the police would never discover that it was him, they all knew Kam'tuta was a weakling, they could insult him and he wouldn't even yell back, he'd just listen. And then in the darkness he could actually see Inácia all dressed in white, laid out in her coffin and her skin even more beautiful, except no one had been able to close her eyes, they had stayed open and big like when she was alive, only they were unlit, empty of their fire, covered instead with *cacimbo*. The worst thing is when you think a lot about your rage the rage gets spent and is over. Slowly the pain left him, a great pity came in its place and he was ready to sleep with his forgiveness of Inácia; but João Miguel, that great fist raised above his head, wouldn't let him. That also hurt because Garrido knew he was a friend, the only one he could usually talk to about what he was feeling inside, even about wanting to kill himself and everything else. That's why it was so hard, his words were stinging in his head again, what he had heard in the darkness,

73

calling him half-a-man. Even him, João Miguel, his friend who had always comforted him saying that what mattered was one's head and that Garrido had a good head, even he could call him a legless cripple. And there was more – he didn't want to take him along on the duck job. Him, Garrido Fernandes, not going along on a duck job! Him, who had already suffered six months for the rest of them because of that theft at a service station! They could shove him aside like this, like an old rag that's only good for the dustbin. That hurt, that hurt a lot, like the words he himself didn't know how he could have said to João Miguel were hurting too, the boy didn't deserve that, but in that moment everything had come out of his mouth without stopping, it wasn't even him any more who was talking, seemed like he was possessed, he just screamed out what the demon in him ordered him to. And if Speedy was going to be angry with him for good? Now that he couldn't even talk to Inácia any more? And Dosreis too, his long-time friend, his respect for him was like for a father, he hadn't even paid any attention, hadn't defended him, just a few weak words when he himself, only he, could convince João Miguel to take him with them too, without old Lóló the job couldn't be done. Why didn't he insist? Why didn't he argue with Speedy, stand up for him?

All these thoughts rolling around in his head were begging him to get up, not just to stay lying down there like that, waiting for something to happen, just like as it so happens. The words he himself had said to João Miguel, to fight, not to surrender, he remembered them now one by one and an even hotter chill ran through him. Right! He would fight! But how? Him, a cripple, passed over for such a simple thing as stealing ducks, a shoemaker without shoes, others knew about him and the white shoemakers would say he was a thief, they wouldn't even give him work during the daytime, how was he going to fight? And if he did fight, with who then? João Miguel, Speedy? No; he had refused to once, he didn't want to hit him with his closed fist, but he wouldn't ever be able to talk with him again, 'cause for sure there'd be trouble. And then too, with a friend fighting wasn't the same thing. He really just wanted to go around with him, to talk, to help, to go on being helped, to keep the *diamba* from taking over the switchman's head for good.

Lomelino? Dosreis was his elder, almost his father – he didn't know his own father, just some whiteman – and also it wasn't all his fault, he directed the jobs but it was João who was their leader. And what's more, Lomelino was an elder, you're not supposed to fight with an elder not even with words, otherwise all the other younger ones would never respect you again.

Inácia? Yes, her, no-good bitch, always making fun, taunting him. But under those insults, the sweet words she would give him sometimes or even those eyes she would fix on him when he'd start talking about the good life he dreamed about, they were like a heavy weight and they won out over the insults, they didn't let him feel the truth, that he really was what the girl was always saying, a weakling.

So who? Each one was good and bad; seen alone he couldn't fight any one of them, it wouldn't be right. Lóló and Speedy had put him aside, but tomorrow, not having run any risks, he would receive half of half the profits for himself and João Miguel never cheated him, that money was sacred he would say. So who was the enemy? Jacó? And suddenly he could see the culprit clearly, the real bandit was that old bad-mannered creature; but then he actually burst out laughing. A man like him and the enemy was a bird? Couldn't be! But the truth was that the idea was growing like grass all through his head and his heart. No, it couldn't be, never! It was true that the *monas* would taunt him 'Kam'tuta, swing your foot' after hearing the parrot, but it was Inácia who taught him, she had made it up. A parrot doesn't think, it only says what it hears, what they tell it. And if the *monandengues* called him that it wasn't really because they were cruel, it was because they would hear the older ones and the parrot screeching it. Best to forgive the creature.

But, then, taking liberties like walking around under Inácia's dress where Garrido wouldn't even look, now isn't that being an enemy? A shameless bird getting more affection than a person? So, was Jacó the enemy? Couldn't be. Poor creature, he's just bad because of what he's taught, it's *sô* Ruas who made him so bad-mannered with those dirty words in Kimbundu, poor thing they didn't even wipe his ass, feathers always filthy, full of chicken lice, he didn't have a perch, he had to sleep in the *mandioqueira* tree, no one ever taught him pretty things; really, he could whistle nicely if left alone, he couldn't be the enemy of a person.

But in the darkness of his room the dirty old parrot Jacó seemed to be his salvation, he would free him of many things, he would serve him to fight all of them. That was it, Jacó would be his weapon. He would kill him, it wouldn't be easy to strangle him, but then he was already old, poor thing, he wasn't of use for anything any more. That would really be the best revenge.

First: Lóló and João Miguel would see how valuable he was, he wasn't just good for standing guard on street corners. All by himself he was going to steal a parrot, a bird that's like a person, could almost talk; he would show them what he was, then they would ask him to please always be their man for stealing birds and he'd refuse.

Second: he would also end those screams of 'Kam'tuta, swing your foot.' If they stopped hearing that cry the *monandengues* would forget it; if he had to he would even shut himself up in his room for a few weeks, pretend he was sick, to give them time to forget that nickname.

Third and most important: that son-of-a-bitch would never be fooling around with Inácia again, stealing the affection meant for a person the way he did.

He laughed, satisfied with his plan; his rage had fled and instead a big though slightly cruel happiness hovered around his mouth. He looked for his tennis shoes in the dark and put them on, put on his shirt, then went out into the night whistling; he could already see Inácia's face waking up in the morning without the parrot, served her right, that bird wouldn't be picking *jingubas* out of her pretty mouth ever again, he wouldn't be tickling her breasts with his neck feathers ever again, looking for the hidden nuts, he wouldn't ever again run from the rain by getting under Inácia's skirt into the warm darkness of her thighs. Never again that son-of-a-bitch!

'*Sukua*'! Then it'll be me! I'll be the parrot!'

As it struck against the walls, his voice, a little hoarse from being quiet all that time, startled him; but then immediately he laughed out into the darkness; they'd see who he was yet, the so-called Kam'tuta of their taunts, he, he himself, Garrido Fernandes, mulatto as it so happens, paralysis as it so happens had ruined his leg, but in his head he was smarter than all the rest of them with two legs!

The night was ugly. Dark, not one star peeking through and the moon was hidden asleep in the smoke of a thick *cacimbo* that looked just like rain. The silence hid the shanties even more and only people like Garrido who lived there could walk along the narrow paths among the yards without bumping into walls and fences. He moved slowly to enjoy every second of the happiness that had come upon him when he saw that all he had to do was grab Jacó, twist his neck and make him disappear forever.

He whistled through the darkness and it seemed like he was imitating on purpose all of Jacó's whistles that'd stayed in his head. The dirt squeaked under his tennis shoes, his crippled leg left a line where he dragged his foot, which looked like the path of a snail. Very softly, from between the thin lips of his narrow mouth, came the limericks he was making up:

> 'Parrot of gold
> acts like a toad.'

He kept on walking, singing his limerick with a dancing beat as it came into his head:

> 'Dumb dirty pest
> Hanged by your neck.'

Through the *cacimbo*, there at the end of the path, the black splotch of the big *mandioqueira* in the Widow's yard came into view. Only then did Garrido's heart beat harder; now that he was arriving the happiness fled, he glanced around, looking into all the dark corners, moving forward more slowly, cautiously.

To open the little wooden gate at the back of the yard near the hen house was a cinch for him. He knew it very well, that was the way he usually ran out when Inácia's madame came home. She didn't like the boy going through the house, she had told the girl that the whole *musseque* knew Garrido was a petty thief and it looked bad that an *assimilada* like herself with a white godmother and everything should be paying attention to a no-good like that cripple. He didn't make a sound when he entered but a rooster gave a small ca-ca-ca then was quiet as it joined in Garrido's silence. He kept walking but even more quietly, he would set down one foot then lift up the other very slowly and put it on the ground, then rest all his weight on it and begin to raise the other foot – this was the way Speedy had taught him, explaining it was how they wanted it done in the army, to make the footsteps of a ghost that the enemy could never hear.

He knew the way well, he didn't need the moon but she did help a bit, piercing a little of the *cacimbo*'s cloth and lighting up the yard. The *mandioqueira* was close by, only three more steps, but he didn't want to hurry, he was enjoying the process to the very full, he couldn't make even one little sound because Inácia usually slept nearby in the small room at the side of the coal shed. Nothing could be seen through the darkness of the leaves and the tree's shadow was a huge black spot on the dimly lit red earth. Only two more steps were left and Kam'tuta took them, calling softly, 'Jacó ... Jacó ...'

On the left side where it was darkest he felt the movement of a straw mat. He stopped, startled, but then didn't hear it again, must have been fear making those noises, just the rustling of the wind in the leaves of the *mandioqueira*.

'Jacó ... Jacó ... Hello! Jacózinho ...'

Now he was touching him, the bird was under his fingers, he passed his hands softly over the few feathers of the parrot's neck, caressing him. He felt him shiver, then take his head out

78

from under one wing. He grabbed him carefully, talking gently just like Inácia did, 'Jacó! Give me your foot ... here, love ... your foot ...'

The stupid bird didn't even move, contented by the tickling and warmth of his words. Kam'tuta put him under his old coat between the lining and his shirt, calmed him and smiled with satisfaction, a happiness spreading through his body. The silly creature was caught; tomorrow he only had to twist his neck and that would be it: his bad luck would be over once and for all when that bird couldn't talk any more. Moving backwards he started to withdraw towards the darkest spot to work his way along the fence planks to the gate he had left open. He set his crippled leg behind him, made an effort, then without looking moved the other leg, already in the air, back carefully, afraid of brushing against a pan since the *massuicas* were close by.

But it wasn't the rocks he touched, oh no. Under his tennis shoes he could feel a large round mass, like an animal, and this form suddenly moved with a big rustling of the straw mat. In the silence Kam'tuta yelped in fear, all the hens burst out cackling, the rooster, awakened, began crowing, the geese acted just like they had gone mad and Garrido, dragging his leg, limped to the gate as fast as he could, clutching his jacket together to hang on to Jacó, at this point he wasn't about to let him go.

With Garrido's fear, the parrot had become very wide awake and was scratching and pecking at his chest, struggling to get free. And finally, right next to the wooden gate, Garrido's heart froze ice cold, colder than the *cacimbo* night, and even without the urge to flee running through his blood his legs moved ahead all by themselves. Because from under the *mandioqueira* tree he had heard Inácia's voice laughing, loud and clear, talking to the man who was lying down there with her, saying don't go, it's not important, I know him, it's just a trick. Tomorrow I'll get back what he came to take away ... Furious, Kam'tuta slammed the wooden gate shut and hurried off into the *cacimbo* that was covering the moon again, more thickly now. In the darkness Inácia's voice was the only hot breath that reached his ears as

79

he fled, 'Kam'tuta, Kam'tut'é, sleep with Jacó, make him a baby!'

And the bird, wide awake and hanging onto Garrido's angry hand for dear life, was still able to screech out the insults he had picked up from hearing his mistress' voice, 'Kam'tuta ... tuta ... swing your foot ... foot ... foot.'

*   *   *

It was lucky when Garrido arrived at the station house that Lomelino wasn't there in the cell, he had gone to see a visitor, otherwise there would have been a fight. But as it was Xico Futa himself was there to receive him, Dosreis' friend knew him as soon as he came in, shamefaced, dragging his leg slowly and hiding from everyone's eyes.

This is how the police behaved: they arrived at his god-mother's house and without asking anyone's permission they barged right in and asked about a lame mulatto boy, Garrido Fernandes, and when he got up to leave his room, his face full of sleep, his blue eyes blinking in fear of the afternoon light, they told him straight away they knew he'd gone with Dosreis, a Cape-Verdian, to rob Ramalho da Silva's yard and had stolen a sack of ducks; Lomelino told everything so it won't help to deny it, better just get your shirt on and let's go.

But Garrido resisted; with his godmother's help he talked, he pleaded, he showed them all around the shanty so they could see that there wasn't anything stolen there; and she swore the boy had gone to sleep early that night, he had even come home looking sick with fever, she herself saw him go into his room, lie down, and she had even heard him coughing, how could he have gone and stolen some ducks?

'I swear it, sô Chief! I myself even asked him: "Gágá, do you need anything," and he answered me: no thanks, just that he was fed up with his life. That's the truth! He can't find a good job, they won't take him with that leg of his ...'

But it was no use, police aren't convinced by words; they just grabbed Garrido soon as he had his trousers on so he wouldn't try to hide in the yard and told him to get a move on. They'd had a complaint, the other had talked, and now they had to take him in and find out the truth. Then Garrido made things even worse. With some kind of idea of saving himself he told them everything about stealing the parrot, he went into his room and brought out the basket where the creature was caged up waiting for the mulatto to wring its neck and throw it into the dustbin.

'Oh, so it's like that, is it? You good-for-nothing! Let's go!'

And then, right in front of his godmother, they had to go and crack him on the neck, then shoved him into the jeep, not paying any attention at all to Garrido's words of defence, 'I swear it, sô Chief! As it so happens his mistress saw me and said herself I could take him. It's just a game of mine!'

Hah! The heart of a policeman is made of stone and they took him all the same; they were even pleased because if the accusation was false then now they had a good excuse anyway.

That was what Garrido told Xico Futa who had bumped into him right away when the mulatto, all depressed, had sat down on the floor wanting to cry and to fight Dosreis, he just couldn't believe the other would do such a thing, lie about him like that. If it had been true, okay, he would understand, but like this it hurt. And straight away he started insulting Dosreis; Xico Futa tried to tell him he was a friend of Lomelino and he knew all about it; Garrido refused to answer him, told him to go away and leave him alone with his rage, and that Cape-Verdian when he came back would just see if he could go around making fun of a person like that. But Xico Futa never backed out when he wanted to help a person and this boy Garrido, well, he felt sorry for him.

'Now listen! You don't solve anything by getting angry. If you attack him when he comes back, it won't help at all. First, Lomelino won't care, he can fight back. Then, the cipaio will come after you with his whip. And all for what?'

'Leave me alone! It's my life! I'm going to fight, I swear I'm

81

going to fight! Why should I let a son-of-a-bitch like that say I stole some ducks?'

'Now listen! Mistakes are made, that's the way it is. You were the only one who knew the job was going to happen. Think about that, Garrido. Dosreis was furious, he thought you had told on him because they didn't let you ...'

Kam'tuta tried to get up, his blue eyes shining in anger. 'That's just it! That's just what I can't accept. It's not the lie about me, no sir. But someone who knows me since I was a *monandengue*, how could he think I'd do such a thing? How? Just tell me! How?'

Well, Xico Futa had to admit that was true, Garrido wasn't all that wrong; but, too, when they caught Lomelino it was night time, he was brought in and immediately there was this thing with Zuzé, you have to understand all this, not just think about yourself. And besides, nothing was going to happen anyway, because Dosreis had already told him he would tell them that the accusations he had made against Garrido were a lie, everything would be all right again, he would spend two or three days here and then they'd send him home.

'Ah, as it so happens with things like this you might be right. But don't forget the parrot! That's the worst thing, *sô* Futa. The very worst! Not because I stole the creature, no. As it so happens I don't care if I stay here a whole week, a whole month in jail. But I didn't get to kill him! I stole him so I could wring the bastard's neck!'

He stopped talking, thinking to himself. Xico Futa lit a cigarette and gave it to him, but Garrido didn't want it, he was only thinking about how now, probably, Inácia had already gone to his godmother's to get the parrot, and how she would come to the police to accuse him, and how they would give that creature back to her. When he got out everything would be just the same as before: Jacó in his tree screeching insults at him, taunting him; Inácia kissing him, letting a dirty old bird do what it wanted; and worst of all Lomelino and João Miguel would never take him back into their group. But it was all Lóló's fault; who told him to lie about his going along with stealing those ducks?

'I swear! I'm going to fight him! You'll see when he gets back here!'

The afternoon came through the window with only a little bit of light from the *cacimbo* sun. The prisoners were everywhere, on the floor and on the wooden bunks; some were sleeping with their eyes closed resting, others with their eyes open letting their thoughts wander. Some were gathered in corners talking softly, exchanging adventures or just everyday things. Xico Futa stretched his long legs along the floor, lit another cigarette and insisted Garrido take it. This time the mulatto accepted and began to smoke. At his side, Futa burst out laughing, first slowly, shaking, trying not to let it all out, then with big white horselaughs until tears came into his eyes; of course the cigarette smoke didn't help that.

'What're you laughing at?'

'Nothing ... nothing ...'

Lie. He was laughing because he could see Garrido Kam'tuta's funny figure lost in the middle of the dark *cacimbo* night, proceeding with great courage just to steal a parrot. He looked into his skinny beardless face and felt a great pity. He said, 'Damn it, brother Garrido! Weren't you afraid to go alone like that to take the parrot? You know, for something really valuable you take some risks. But a creature that's no good for anything ...'

Xico Futa's voice was good, like Lomelino's when he wanted to be his father, or like João Miguel when he would talk about what happens in life and put questions so Garrido would talk about his own ideas. He laughed at Xico and felt a little vanity with those words of praise from a strong man like him. True, he hadn't even thought much about it when he made up his mind, it was just his fury at the parrot that moved his legs.

'Oh, I guess I did it 'cause I knew him and the house and the yard pretty well.' He made it seem less than it was on purpose so he could listen to the other go on praising his courage. It would be even better if Dosreis and João could hear him so they would forget that crazy idea of not wanting to take him on their jobs, of wanting to toss him aside like a piece of rubbish. But now Xico Futa was going on to other matters.

'Hey, listen. You still angry with Lomelino?'

Garrido really wanted to say yes, that he was just waiting to fight him, but his mouth refused, if he said that it would be a lie. Xico Futa had ruined everything inside him with his words, the cigarette and his friendship, and all he could get out was a mumbled, 'Oh! Leave me alone!'

'No, Garrido. Now listen! Lomelino will be back in a minute, he's just gone to see a visitor ... I don't want the two of you to start arguing. Okay?'

'No, damn it! It's not okay ...'

He was lying and you could tell he was straight away. When Zuzé opened the door to send Dosreis in, Garrido didn't even get up. It was Xico who jumped to his feet, ready to grab either one of them if they tried to fight. But Lomelino was startled, and with the bundle of things to eat pressed against his chest and his clothes in his other hand, he just blinked his tired old eyes, glancing at the boy's bent head, his fair curly hair, his shoulders hunched up not wanting to be straight and he couldn't move from his spot. He looked for Xico's eyes, but Futa pretended he was watching the sun trying to come through the window. All alone, with no one's eyes seeking his own, with no words from anyone, Dosreis felt the truth of what he had done; even though he had taken it back later it didn't matter: Garrido was there now too, a prisoner, and he himself was the stool pigeon. He said slowly, 'Garrido?'

Kam'tuta raised his blue eyes, they were small and cold now, just like ice.

'You ... er ... are you angry with me?'

Not a word, nothing. Just those eyes fixed on his face, surprised, just like the boy had never seen him before, like he was a stranger, just anyone. He felt a pain in his belly when that look pierced into him like that, he wouldn't forgive him; then he thought of something and tried it, 'Listen, Gágá! Mília sent along a bean stew for you. She knows how much you like it.'

Emília was Lomelino's wife. She was always treating Kam'tuta like he was only ten years old, she liked his sad little-boy manner very much, and she enjoyed speaking to him in the creole words of Cape Verde, talking about the life of her island. He wanted to hear everything, wonderingly, as if what she was doing was making up a pretty tale and not talking about the miseries of life on those islands.

'Did you hear, Gágá? Emília . . .'

But going on wasn't going to help. Garrido had already stood up; these words from Lóló had caused a wanting-to-be-happy to show in his eyes and so that the Cape-Verdian couldn't see this – in his anger he wasn't going to show content on his face – he moved very slowly towards the barred iron gate, drawing on the rest of his cigarette. Lomelino made a move to follow him, but Xico Futa grabbed his arm, pulling him back, 'Let him go, *compadre*! Let his anger go away by itself.'

They sat down on the wooden bunk at the back, Xico's spot, and began to undo the package of things: a pot of palm oil bean stew, manioc meal, fried fish, banana and bread. *Musseque* people's food. The pot was still warm, even though a lot of time had passed since *nga* Mília had left her house so far away up there. Xico Futa started to eat straight away, he put the fish on the bread and began to bite into it with his strong teeth. But Dosreis couldn't; he was looking at the food, his head down, the shame he felt when he came in and saw Garrido's eyes was even greater now with Mília's food in front of him. He took hold of Xico's hand and said, 'Call him, brother Xico!'

Futa smiled, 'Hey, Garrido! Come on and eat, we're waiting for you!'

Leaning on the bars, looking out at the corridor with empty eyes, Kam'tuta shivered. Saliva came into his mouth, he thought about the yellow bean stew shining in its pot, the manioc meal waiting to be mixed in, and hunger made his mind run away from its former thoughts. But he didn't turn around. In his heart some of his rage was still boiling over the accusation, even though he had seen clearly Lomelino's sad, repentant: face when he came in, he wasn't going to eat with a stool pigeon.

He spat into the corridor, mumbled some words even he didn't know what and tried to get back into his old thoughts again. It was hard, the bean stew was the only thing filling his mind right now, the things he had thought about before were running away, those ideas he had had that his name would be in the newspaper, in a report about the theft of the parrot Jacó, and how maybe he would even hold out just to taunt Inácia, to ask her if she had ever had her name in the newspaper and, who knows, maybe they would even come to take his picture to put in it ...

But another bunch of words hit him. From the back the Cape-Verdian Lomelino, angry now, was shouting, 'Kam'tuta, man! We're not going to get on our knees, you know! Come on over here and eat, damn it!'

Garrido smiled and with the foolishness of friendship he went over to them.

*　　*　　*

So that's my tale. If it's pretty or if it's ugly, only those who can read can say. But I swear that's how they told it and I won't let anyone doubt Dosreis, who has a wife and two sons and steals ducks and who wasn't allowed to get an honest job; Garrido Kam'tuta, crippled from paralysis, made fun of even by a parrot; Inácia Domingas, a sassy young girl who thinks the servant of a white man is white – 'm'bika a mundele, mundele uê'; Zuzé, police assistant, who has no orders to be nice; João Speedy, smoker of diamba trying to forget what he always remembers; Jacó, poor little musseque parrot, they only teach him dirty things and he doesn't even have a perch or anything ...

And that's the truth, even if none of it ever happened.

THE TALE
OF
THE HEN AND THE EGG

For Amorim and his ngoma:
vibrant hearts of our land.

The tale of the hen and the egg happened in the *musseque* of Sambizanga, in this our land of Luanda.

The hour was four.

Sometimes, where the sun ends its day in the sea, a small, fat black cloud appears and it runs across the blue sky and as it runs it starts getting bigger and spreads out arms, arms which become more and more arms, each one getting thinner and less black than the one before, until the hurrying spread of the arms of the cloud across the sky looks like the leafy branches of an ancient *mulemba* tree with its whiskers of multi-coloured leaves dried up by the brightness of the sun; and finally when no one knows any more how they were born or where they began or even where they end, these crazy daughters of the cloud rushing over the city release the hot heavy water they carry, laughing with long twisted lightning flashes and speaking in the deep voice of their thunder. In this way did the confusion begin on a quiet afternoon.

Sô Zé the shopkeeper saw *nga* Zefa pass by dragging along the child Beto and warning him not to start with those lies or else she would put *jindungo* on his tongue. But the young one kept answering back, 'I swear to Christ, Mama! I really saw her. It's Cabiri!'

He was telling the truth for all the women clearly saw a fat hen with small white and black feathers imprisoned underneath an upside-down basket, looking out suspiciously at everyone. That was the reason *nga* Zefa had insulted Bina, calling her a thief and a witch, saying she wanted to steal the hen, and although you could already see the neighbour's belly big with the child inside, they started to fight.

It was the child Xico who had found out; he was playing with the younger Beto doing those tricks Grandpa Petelu taught them of imitating the talk of the animals, confusing them, and when they came into Mama Bina's yard they stopped in surprise.

She didn't have a brood, so how come you could hear her voice making peep, peep, peep, hen-calling sounds, and the noise of corn falling on the swept ground? But Beto remembered something, the words of his mother fussing at his father when seven o'clock he was back from work.

'I'll bloody her nose, João, if she keeps teaching the hen to lay there!'

Miguel João was always ready with an excuse. He said the woman went around with that belly of hers and you know, sometimes it's just one of these fits women have, doesn't help to make a big fuss if the hen always comes back to our coop and you get the eggs . . . But *nga* Zefa wasn't satisfied, she sneered at her man calling him a weakling and swore if that shameless thing laid a hand on the hen there'd be a fight.

'Enough, Zefa, what the hell,' soothed Miguel, 'after all, the woman's carrying a child, her man's in jail and you still want to yell at her? That's not right!'

So *nga* Zefa just kept a very close eye on the hen every day, watching her scratch her way through the dirt, pecking, looking for insects to eat, but in the end her path was always the same, like she'd been bewitched: between two fallen planks Cabiri would enter the neighbour's yard and Zefa would see her pecking happily away in the shade of the fresh *mandioqueira* trees, maybe Bina was even giving her corn or millet. All Zefa could see were the kernels falling on the ground and first the hen looking in surprise at the door of the shanty where this food was coming from, then beginning to pick it up, grain by grain, unhurried, like she knew very well there was no other creature there in the yard to squabble with her over the kernels. All this *nga* Zefa didn't fuss about even though in her heart she feared the hen would get used to it there. But she decided the creature was eating well and, after all, she'd return in the morning to lay her egg in the little hen-coop at the back of her own yard.

But there was bad luck this afternoon. All through the morning Cabiri went strolling around the yard, in the street, in the shade, in the sun, her beak open, shaking her head now on one side, now on the other, singing softly in her throat ... but she didn't lay her egg. It was like she kept looking for a better spot, so *nga* Zefa opened the hen-coop door, fixed up the nest just right, even put another egg in it ... but again nothing happened. The hen wanted to make fun of her, her little yellow eyes taunting while her throat sang,

> ... *ngala ngó ku kakela*
>
> *ká ... ká ... ká ... kakela, kakela ...*

And so, when the child Beto came telling how Cabiri was imprisoned underneath a basket at *nga* Bina's shanty and how he and Xico even saw the woman giving her corn, *nga* Zefa knew: that wretched hen had laid the egg in her neighbour's yard. She went out, with her thin body bent over and the rage she'd been saving up a long time rising to her tongue. *Sô* Zé the shopkeeper stayed in his doorway to watch because you could really see the fury in that woman's face.

What a fight! There was scratching, hair-pulling, name-calling like thief, goat, witch. Xico and Beto escaped to a corner and only came out when the two women were pulled apart. Cabiri was covered by the big basket but she could see out like a prisoner from behind bars. She watched all the people gathered there talking, her small eyes round and quiet, her beak closed. Near her, placed deliberately on some grass, a pretty white egg was shining, looking like it was still warm and enraging *nga* Zefa. The fighters had finally been separated and now the curious Beto and Xico kept trying to penetrate the circle of people to watch the argument continue.

Nga Zefa, hands on her waist, her eyes flashing with rage, stretched the thin bones of her body towards her neighbour, 'You think I don't know you, Bina? That's what you think? With that face of yours looking so smart. But we know! We know you're nothing but a thief!'

The plump young neighbour rubbed a flat hand on her swollen belly, her face breaking into a smile, then calmly turning to the others, she said, 'Ay, look at that! She's still going on at me. You came into my house, you came into my yard, you even wanted to fight! *Sukuama!* And me with this belly! Don't you have any respect at all?'

'Don't you try your tricks on me, Bina! Excuses! You wanted to steal Cabiri and her egg from me!'

'Hah! Steal Cabiri and the egg from you? The egg's mine!'

Zefa jumped at her, poking her finger in Bina's face, 'Your egg? Shit! It's my hen laid it!'

'Right, but she laid it in my yard!'

There were murmurs of approval and disapproval among the neighbours, everyone was talking at once. But old Bebeca went up and tugged at Zefa's arm, her wisdom speaking, 'Calm down! The head speaks, the heart hears! What're you insulting her like that for? Nobody understands if everyone talks at the same time. Each one has her say and we'll see who's right. We're people, *sukua'*, not animals!'

A quiet approval supported Grandma's words and everyone waited. *Nga* Zefa felt her fury leaving her, she saw the faces of her friends waiting, Bina's protruding belly, and to get her courage back she called to her son, 'Beto, come here!' Then excusing herself, she turned again to the people and spoke, still upset, 'It's just that the *monandengue* saw ...'

Slowly, like she was afraid of the words, Miguel João's woman spoke of how for a long time now she was seeing the hen go into the other woman's yard every day and how she already knew this confusion would happen; she clearly saw her neighbour wooing Cabiri with food. And today – the boy saw and so did Xico – that thief caught the hen by insisting on giving her corn and put her underneath the basket to get the egg. Cabiri was hers, everyone knew that and even Bina wasn't denying it; Cabiri laid the egg so the egg was hers too.

Some of the women nodded their heads yes, others no. One girl began talking to Beto and Xico, asking them questions, but Grandma ordered them all to be quiet.

'Now you talk, Bina!'

'What more do I have to say, Grandma? *Sukuama*, everyone already heard the truth. The hen's Zefa's, I don't want her. But then her hen comes into my yard, eats my corn, pecks at my *mandioqueira* trees, sleeps in my shade, then lays the egg here and the egg is hers? *Sukua'!* It was my corn made the egg. If it wasn't for me doing the feeding, the poor thing wouldn't have the strength to sing. Now the egg is mine, mine, you hear!' She wriggled her body around, slapped her bottom, then pulled her eyelid down with her finger, laughing mischievously at her neighbour who was again in the middle of the circle pointing to the frightened hen behind the woven straw of the old basket.

'Look at her! She's mine, that thief even said so. There's the grass, there's the egg. Feel it! Feel it, it's still warm! And she's saying the egg is hers? Liar! The hen's mine and so's the egg!'

Once again they all spoke, each one with her opinion, making a noise which mingled with the rustling of the *mandioqueiras* and made Cabiri so frightened that she started hopping around everywhere, putting her head up and down, and turning around to look at the women. But no one paid her any attention, except Beto and Xico, little friends of every creature, who know their voices and their needs. They looked at the basket and saw how the poor thing wanted to get out, to be free, and how no one would ever let her out with all this confusion.

Now, looking for sympathy, *nga* Bina turned her pitiful eyes on the crowd and whined, 'That's right, my friends. I'm the one who's so clever. Every day she saw me giving the hen corn and she didn't say anything, not even thank you, she just let me go on doing it! Doesn't that count? Well, what does she want? The hen's fat with my corn and she's going to eat the egg?'

Turning away from the other women – only women and children were around because at that hour the men were working and only loafers and pimps were asleep in the shanties – Grandma interrupted, 'Now then, Bina, was it for you the hen was to lay the egg?'

The girl smiled, glancing at the hen's owner, then defended herself to the faces, some friendly, others quiet with thought.

'Oh damn! Lots of you already been with your belly swollen. Grandma herself knows how when this urge to eat something comes on there's nothing you can do about it. The child in my belly keeps wanting an egg. What can I do, just tell me?'

'But the egg's not yours! The hen's mine, so's the egg! You could ask me! If I want to, I'll give it to you and if I don't want to I won't!' *Nga* Zefa was furious again. Bina's talking in those quiet gentle tones about all that business of the child in her belly and the hunger was attacking the heart of the people; if she went on talking with those clever eyes and her hand always rubbing her round belly under her dress, Zefa would lose, the people would have pity on Bina, excuse her hunger for an egg and would say it wasn't her fault . . . She turned to Grandma. The old woman was drawing on the little cigar in her mouth, blowing out the smoke and spitting.

'Well, Grandma? Say something, you're our elder.'

Everyone was quiet, their eyes on the wise old wrinkled face. Only Beto and Xico, stooping down next to the basket, were talking to the hen, watching her small frightened feathers tremble with the wind, her round eyes looking at their friendly smiles.

Pulling her cloth up over her shoulder, old Bebeca began, 'My friends, the snake is rolled around the water jug. If I grab the jug, the snake bites; if I kill the snake, the jug breaks! You, Zefa, are right. The hen's yours, the egg from its belly's yours. But Bina also has her right. The egg was laid in her yard, the hen ate her corn. Better we ask sô Zé . . . he's white . . .'

Sô Zé, the scrawny one-eyed shopkeeper, was already on his way to see what the commotion was about. At that hour the *quitanda* was empty; not having any customers he could leave it.

'Sô Zé, please listen to this and then give your opinion. My friend here . . .' But everyone started interrupting Grandma. Ohhh no, each one should tell her own story, that way no one can say later the old woman cheated, talking up one side better than the other. Sô Zé agreed, went up closer to the protesters and fixing his pretty blue eye on Zefa's face, he asked, 'Well then, what happened?'

Nga Zefa began to tell but in the end she was keeping away from the part about spotting her neighbour giving out the corn every day so Grandma added, 'Go on, tell that you saw her putting out corn for Cabiri every day.'

'Right! I forgot. I didn't do it on purpose, I swear!'

Sô Zé, his back all hunched up, patiently put on a smile and took Bina's arm. 'That's enough! Now I know everything. You say that the hen laid in your back yard, that the corn she ate is yours and therefore you want the egg. Right?'

With these friendly sounding words of *sô* Zé, the young woman began to laugh. She felt the egg would be hers now, all she needed to do was puncture it, two little holes, suck and then lick her lips right in the loser's face. But when she looked at him again, *sô* Zé was serious, his face a mask full of lines and ugly holes where only the pretty blue of his eye shone out from deep inside just like when he was behind the counter looking at the pans of the scale when he weighed, the measures when he measured, to weigh less and measure less than was due.

'Listen here!' He spoke at *nga* Bina and her face immediately lost its grin, but her hand continued caressing her belly. 'That corn you gave Cabiri . . . is it some of the corn I sold you yesterday?'

'That's right, *sô* Zé! I'm glad you understand . . .'

'Ah yes? The corn I sold you on credit yesterday? And you say that egg is yours? Aren't you ashamed!'

He put his skinny hand on Grandma's shoulder and with an evil, mocking grin he spoke slowly, 'Madame Bebeca, the egg is mine! Tell them to give me the egg. The corn still hasn't been paid for.'

These words brought on a loud rumbling, then threats, and the women surrounded the shopkeeper, insulting him, shoving his scrawny twisted body, driving him back to his house.

'Get out of here, you white shit!'

'Damn thief! Just look at him!'

When he went back into his *quitanda*, laughing and smug, Zefa screamed out, 'Sukuama! Did you see that? Not enough you cheat on the scales, is it? Is it, you greedy white bastard?!'

But the matter was still not resolved.

When the laughter and noise over the confusion with that whiteman stopped, nga Zefa and nga Bina looked at Grandma, waiting for the old woman to settle things. Beto and Xico went back to the basket and stayed there gazing at Cabiri again. The creature had become frightened with all the noise of the squabbling with sô Zé, but now feeling a fresh breeze tickling her beneath her wings and feathers, she took advantage of the silence and began to sing.

'Listen, Beco,' whispered Xico, 'just listen to her song!' And they burst out laughing at the hen's singing. They knew the words very well because old Petelu had taught them to them.

'Quiet, boys! Just what're you laughing at?' Grandma's voice was almost angry.

'Beto, come here! You still laughing, is that it? They want to steal your mother's egg and you're laughing?'

The child ducked so they couldn't box his ears or slap him, but Xico stuck up for him. 'No, Grandma. It's the hen, she's talking.'

'Oh! Don't you think I know animals talk with crazy people? And just what's she saying? She saying who owns the egg?'

'Maybe, Grandma. It's sô Petelu who really knows. He taught me!'

Grandma Bebeca smiled, her eyes sparkling, and to take away some of the anger from each face, she continued to tease the child. 'Then what's she saying? Could be she's talking about the egg.'

Suddenly Beto left his hiding place in the mandioqueira tree and said before Xico could even begin, 'The hen talks like this, Grandma:

> 'Ngëxile kua ngana Zefa
> Ngala ngó ku kakela
> Ká ... ká ... ká ... kakela, kakela ...'

95

And then Xico, with his squeaky voice, went over to his friend and the two of them began to sing just like Cabiri who became all confused, wriggling her head, hearing the other hen but not seeing it.

> '. . . *ngëjile kua ngana Bina*
> *Ala kiá ku kuata*
> *kua . . . kua . . . kua . . . kuata, kuata!*'

And they began to pretend they were hens pecking at the corn on the ground. Grandma scolded them to be quiet. *Nga* Zefa started to chase after Beto and the two friends went running out of the yard.

But they didn't stay out more than a minute. All excited, Xico came back first to give Grandma Bebeca the news. 'Grandma, here comes Azulinho!'

'Call him, Xico, don't let him get away!'

Everyone was smiling now. *Nga* Zefa and *nga* Bina let out a deep breath and some of the wrinkles of worry about this whole thing slipped away from Grandma's face. Azulinho's fame was great in the *musseque*, there just wasn't any other boy as clever as him, only sixteen years old but it didn't matter, he was the pride of Mama Fuxi, *sô* Father from the seminary even said he was going to send him to study in Rome. And even though the other *monas* and some older kids made fun of him because he was weak and would cry over one playful shove, when it was time for serious talk, could be religion, could be Latin, could be mathematics, no one doubted Azulinho would know. João Pedro Capita was his name and they nicknamed him Azulinho because of that used blue suit he would never throw away, hot or cold, he always wore it well starched and ironed.

Grandma called him over and brought him into the middle of the women to hear how it all happened. The boy listened, blinking his eyes behind his glasses while pulling the sides of his coat down. You could see in his face he was flustered in the midst of so many women, a lot of them still only girls, and *nga* Bina's round swollen belly right in front of him made him stretch out his hands without meaning to just like he was afraid the woman would touch him with that part of her body.

'Listen good, child. This thing already made lots of trouble, you know, now you've got to help us. Mama Fuxi says you know everything there is to know!'

Hiding a vain smile and joining his hands together like he was already sô Father himself, João Pedro spoke. 'I say unto thee, Madame justice is blind and carries a sword.' He cleared his throat in search of the words and everyone saw his face smile with the ideas being born, coming into his head to say what he wanted. 'Thou temptest me with flattery! And, as Jesus Christ to the scribes, I say unto thee: do not tempt me! And I ask thee to show me the egg, as He asked for the coin.'

It was Beto with all his experience who took the egg without frightening Cabiri, she liked to peck when they did this but he sang to her softly what he'd learned about talking to animals. Turning the egg over in his white palm, Azulinho went on just like he was talking only to himself, no one even understanding much of what he was saying but he wasn't interrupted; after all the boy was famous.

'Neither the image of Caesar, nor the image of God!' He raised his weak eyes behind his glasses and looked first to Zefa, then to Bina, concluding, 'Neither the mark of your hen, Zefa, nor the mark of your corn, Bina. I can not give to Caesar what is Caesar's, nor to God what is God's. Only Father Julio himself knows the truth. So, Grandma Bebeca, I shall take the egg to him!'

A murmur of approval came from the group but nga Zefa wouldn't have it. She wasn't going to let that egg get away after so much fuss! Jumping in front of the boy, she grabbed the egg from his hand and smacked her lips against her teeth. 'Sukuama! Will you look at that? Now he wants to take the egg away to sô Father! Oh no you don't! You can't have it and don't you dare try to trick me with your learning, even if I don't know how to read or write, it doesn't matter!'

Azulinho, a little angry, made a gesture to say goodbye, bowed, then raised his hands with the fingers placed like sô

Father and left talking to himself, 'Sinners! They wanted to tempt me. Women are the devil!'

With night not far off the women remembered the dinner to be made – when the men returned from work they wouldn't be accepting any excuses about the confusion over the hen – and some of them went off to their shanties, talking about how maybe Grandma wouldn't be able to resolve things without there being another fight. But *nga* Zefa still wasn't going to give up; she wanted to take the egg and the hen. Grandma Bebeca had been given the egg for safekeeping, wouldn't be any surprise at all if an angry woman broke it right then and there. Only poor little Cabiri, tired of all this, was lying down again in the nest of grass, waiting.

At that moment *nga* Mília spotted *sô* Vitalino at the other end of the street getting off the bus.

'*Aiuê*, bad luck! Here comes that man to collect from me again! João still hasn't come back from Lukala, how'm I going to pay? I'm getting out of here! See you later.' She sneaked through the hole in the yard's fence, trying to keep out of the old man's sight.

That whole side of the *musseque* was afraid of *sô* Vitalino. On those days at the end of the month, the man would get off the bus with his silver-headed walking stick, old brown suit, and heavy khaki-coloured helmet, to collect the rents for the shanties he owned there. And he let no one off. Didn't matter if he discovered the man of the house lying on a straw mat eaten up by disease, he would always think up some friend of his from the police or administration to help chase up the unfortunates. This month he'd come early to collect the rent and only from *nga* Mília did he accept any excuse. The truth is everyone knew her man, a stoker with the C.F.L. Railway, was in Malange, but the old man had other ideas in his head. He liked to grab hold of Emília's pretty round arm, colour of coffee and milk, and when he spoke, slobbering through the holes in his teeth, he would say that she didn't have to worry because he knew very well she was a serious woman. He would ask permission to enter the shanty and drink a tin cup of fresh water from the jug, pet the children and always left with the same talk. *Nga* Mília wasn't sure where the old man's friendship stopped and the threats began.

'Take care, Madame Emília! You're a young woman and this life of work doesn't suit you ... So I'll let you off this month and come back in a week, but think with your head. Wouldn't you rather live in Terra Nova in a house with a yard of fruit trees, and no one to bother you with the rent at the end of the month? Think about it!'

Nga Mília would pretend she couldn't hear, but in her heart her rage wanted her man to be there when that sneaky old man talked such rubbish so he would punch that pig's snout ...

Seeing the landlord with his walking stick stumbling through the dirt, his heavy shoes dragging along, Grandma Bebeca thought she must save Emília and the best thing would be to get the old man's attention.

'Good afternoon, *sô* Vitalino!'

'Good afternoon, Madame!'

'Bless you, Grandpa Vitalino,' the other women repeated in chorus with Bebeca to sweet-talk the old man.

Xico and Beto had already run to grab his stick and helmet and were walking around him asking for what no child had yet received from that greedy man.

'Gimme five pennies!'

'Five pennies, Grandpa Lino! For a *quiqüerra*!'

The old man stopped to wipe his forehead with a big red handkerchief which he then folded up carefully and put back into his coat pocket.

'Good afternoon, ladies!' and his little beady eyes searched every face for the face he wanted.

Grandma started: 'It's a good thing you came, *sô* Vitalino! Give us your opinion about these matters. My friends here are saying ...' She spoke slowly and no one interrupted her. *Sô* Vitalino was landlord of so many shanties he could live without working, his children even went to the high school. It was only

99

Grandma who could make conversation with him as an equal. He wouldn't take it from the others, he'd be sure to get angry with them.

'You mean, Madame Bebeca, the egg was laid here in the yard of the girl Bina, is that it?'

'That's right!' smiled Bina.

Taking off his helmet, *sô* Vitalino looked into Zefa's angry face with the eyes of a crow and taking hold of her arm, he mocked, 'Zefa, girl! Do you know whose shanty that is where your neighbour Bina lives?'

'Huh? It's yours!'

'And do you also know that your hen laid an egg in my shanty's yard? Who gave the permission?'

'*Elá!* Doesn't help to turn things around like that, *sô* Vitalino . . .'

'Shut up!' shouted the old man. 'Is the shanty mine or not?'

Now the women could see the direction *sô* Vitalino was taking. They began to talk back, some saying to others – wouldn't you know letting the greedy old man decide, that would be the result! *Nga* Bina even taunted him, by coming right up to the old man and propping up her fat belly on him like she wanted to push him out of the yard.

'Didn't I pay the rent, tell me, didn't I, *sô* Vitalino?'

'That's right, my girl, you paid! But rent isn't a shanty and it isn't a yard! These are always mine even if you pay, understand?'

The women got even more angry with these tricks, but Bina still tried to convince him. 'Look here, *sô* Vitalino, the shanty is yours, I'm not saying it isn't. But when people pay rent at the end of the month, that's it! They become the owner, isn't that right?'

Old Vitalino laughed, showing his little yellow teeth, but he didn't agree. 'You have the craziest ideas! But it doesn't matter, the egg is mine! It was laid in my shanty! I'd better go call my friend from the police.'

Everyone already knew him and his threats and the older girls *uatobaram*, whooping insults at him. Xico and Beto went on pestering him from all sides trying to get some money and Grandma along with *nga* Bina came up to push him into the street, half in fun, half serious. Seeing him go off towards *nga* Mília's shanty, dragging his feet through the red dirt and leaning on his stick, old Bebeca warned him, 'Don't waste your time, *sô* Vitalino! Emília left for the house of her friend ... he's with the police. You can't fool around with him!'

And the laughter from every mouth stayed in the air to chase after the twisted flustered figure of the landlord Vitalino.

It was already past five o'clock and the sun was changing from white and yellow to red, that colour which it paints on the sky and the clouds and the leaves of the trees when it's going to sleep in the middle of the sea, leaving the night for the stars and the moon. When *sô* Vitalino was noisily sent away, it seemed the affair would never be settled. *Nga* Zefa, after so much anger, silently looked at Cabiri underneath the basket, but Bina still wanted to convince the neighbours that only she had the right to keep the egg.

'But it's true, I'm not lying. When these urges come on us we have to respect them, don't we? ...' While she was talking everyone looked towards the voice of a woman shouting insults. It came from the other side of the yard, from the shanty of the prostitute Rosalia. The neighbours were amazed, for a long time no confusion had gone on over there but it seemed this afternoon was cursed with bad luck. In the doorway where her body could be seen, old now but still good, her full breasts peeping through the slip, Rosalia was shouting, 'Get out, man! Already five-thirty and you slept the whole afternoon! You think I'm your father or what? Get out, you good-for-nothing, go look for work!'

Her man Lemos never said anything when it was time for her to get ready to receive her friends and to drive him out of the shanty – the whole *musseque* knew what was going on, seems he alone pretended he wasn't understanding where the food money came from. He would put his hands in the pockets of his wrinkled trousers and pulling his sick left leg, fat as an *imbondeiro* tree, he'd drag his tennis shoes through the dirt as he went looking around the shops for a bit of work to pay for his liquor and cigarettes and maybe a squabble or two he could settle.

It was just that settling cases was his life. In the past, before the drinking that ruined his health, *sô* Artur Lemos worked in the notary office. You could find very thick books in his house, penal proceedings, civil proceedings, official bulletins, everything just like the house of a lawyer. And when the people got frustrated with the bureaucracy, it was *sô* Artur who helped them.

And even now when the neighbours talked with Rosalia while she waited in the doorway for her customers, no one could make fun of her man. She deceived him with everyone, at times she even called the *monandengues* in to do things the older ones wouldn't, but she was like a cat with its back up when anyone insulted her husband.

'There's not another man like him! You're all just jealous. It's true his body's rotten, not good for anything, but his head's good and there's no one else has his learning!'

And you must believe that she didn't let anyone meddle with his books, even dusty and full of spider webs she'd still show them off. 'See, see! All that's in his head. And your men? In bed they're smart but in their heads there's only shit!'

She'd laugh and shrug her shoulders. 'For the bed you can always get someone. And what's more, they even pay. But find someone with a head like his? Not likely!'

The neighbours would make fun of him, they'd say he taught her those words so they couldn't call him a cuckold, but Rosalia paid no attention. Not even when the children, bored with their games, would run after her man, pestering him with his nickname.

'Twenty-five lines! Twenty-five lines!'

They were magic words because for every case the first thing *sô* Lemos would say was, 'We'll do up a twenty-five-liner and the case is finished!'

But if he'd get the money for the twenty-five-line paper, he'd often go drink it up with Francesinho, Quirino, Kutatuji and other good-for-nothings like them in some *quitanda* closer to São Paulo.

Well, just at the hour when Grandma was about to give up, they saw *sô* Artur Lemos himself and they ran to call him over. A man with such experience, maybe he could resolve the matter. Warning Beto and Xico not to start pestering the old man, Grandma, with the help of the interested parties, presented the facts.

New life entered the ruined body of the former notary assistant. His chest breathed straight out, his eyes stopped watering so much and when he moved he didn't even limp. He opened his arms and began to push people around, you here, you there, be quiet; then, with Grandma Bebeca in front of him, he put *nga* Bina on his left and *nga* Zefa on his right and scratching his nose, he began.

'From what we've seen and having heard the relator and the parties, this deals with a case of property litigation, with bases in customary law.'

The women looked at each other, alarmed, but no one said a word.

Twenty-five lines continued, speaking now to *nga* Zefa, 'You say the hen is yours?'

'Yes, *sô* Lemos.'

'Do you have a certificate of ownership?'

'Do I have what?'

'Certificate, Madame! Certificate of ownership! A receipt that proves the hen is yours.'

Nga Zefa laughed. '*Sukuama!* There's no one in the *musseque* doesn't know Cabiri's mine, *sô* Lemos. Receipt for what?'

'Your purchase, woman! So we can prove foremost that the hen is yours!'

'Damn! That man ... purchase? So if the hen was born to me from another hen in my yard, how is it I'm going to be having a receipt?'

Impatiently, *sô* Lemos made a gesture for her to be quiet and muttered to no one in particular: 'That's it! How can people want to have justice done if they don't even get the documents they need?'

Scratching his nose again, he looked to *nga* Bina who was smiling, pleased with the old man, and asked, 'And can you show the receipt for the corn? No? Then how am I going to say who's right? How? Without documents, without proof of anything? Well?'

He looked straight into the faces of all the people, turned his eyes to Beto and Xico stooping near the hen's basket, then took the egg from Grandma Bebeca.

'You, Madame Bina, we are going to place a formal accusation against your neighbour for intromission into another's property with transfer of portions from the same ... that is, the corn!'

Nga Bina opened her mouth to talk but he went on, 'As for you, Madame Zefa, we shall formally petition your neighbour for attempted theft and usufruct of that theft! ... I need five *escudos* from each of you for paper.'

A great burst of laughter covered the last few words and when the laughing was over Grandma still wanted the answer from him. 'But *sô* Lemos, what do you say? Who's right?'

'I don't know, Madame! Without proceedings for a judgment, justice can not be known. We'll make the petitions ...'

Everyone kept on laughing so Beto and Xico immediately took the opportunity to start having fun. Defeated by the laughter and seeing that he wasn't going to get the money to drink with his friends, *sô* Lemos, being shoved away by Grandma who was almost crying she was laughing so hard, tried one last time.

'Wait, listen! I'll take the egg, I'll take it to my friend the judge and he'll give the sentence.'

'The egg, my ass!' *Nga* Zefa screamed at him in fury. Time had passed, talk and more talk, and nothing resolved and with nonsense like this it wouldn't be surprising if that bold-faced Bina ended up eating the egg.

From the street they could hear *sô* Lemos' hoarse voice as he threw stones at Beto and Xico who were still pestering him. Raising his weak fist the old man yelled at them, 'Ill-mannered! No-goods! Delinquents!'

Then, stopping and filling his chest with air, he hurled the word that was dancing in his head, that word he had read in the papers, 'Gangsters!' And happy with that final insult, he left by way of the twisted paths of the *musseque*, dragging his swollen leg along behind him.

When the neighbours saw that not even *sô* Lemos could resolve the issue and they started to feel the fresh wind blowing and the sun sink closer to the sea way beyond the upper city, they began to say it'd be better to wait for the men to come back from work to settle things. *Nga* Bina didn't agree.

'Oh sure! But my man's in jail and who's going to defend me?'

But it was *nga* Zefa who was really enraged and, jostling old Bebeca out of her way, she moved furiously towards the basket to get the hen. And now the battle began again: Bina caught hold of her dress, ripping it at the shoulder, Zefa gave her a good slap, and they grabbed at each other, scratching, punching, and insulting.

'Thief! She-goat! So you want my egg, do you?'

'*Aiuê*, help! She's beating me, a pregnant woman!'

The confusion grew with all the women trying to separate the two fighters who were even trying to kick each other. Beto and Xico were laughing over in the corner of the yard where they'd dragged Cabiri who, more and more upset, was lifting her neck and moving her head without looking at anything and only the kids could understand her ka, ka, ka. Now in the middle of the battle no one knew who was holding on to who, it seemed that everyone was busy fighting, all you could hear were screams, moans, and curses mixed up with the clucking of the frightened hen, the snickers of the *monandengues*, the wind in the leaves of the *mandioqueira* trees and those sounds which fill

105

the *musseque* when night is coming and the people who work Downtown return to their shanties. That was why no one was aware of the arrival of the patrol.

Only when the sergeant began hitting their backs did they quieten down and begin to rearrange their cloths, their head wraps, and to rub their bruises. Two soldiers had come in behind their officer without anyone's permission and now one on each side of the group they held up their white clubs, threatening and laughing. But the sergeant, a short, fat, sweaty man, had taken off his steel helmet and was shouting, 'You bunch of cows! What the hell is this? Huh? What happened?'

No one answered, just some grunts. Grandma Bebeca took a step forward.

'Can't you hear, you trouble-makers? What is this here? A meeting?'

'Huh! Meeting about what?' Grandma, angry, snapped back.

'Come on, little Granny, let's have it. Why were they fighting? Quick! Otherwise I'll take everyone to the police station!'

Grandma saw in the soldier's eyes he was speaking the truth so she looked for help from the other women. But their faces said nothing, they were looking down at the ground, up in the air, over to the corner where Beto and Xico were still with the basket, and at the two soldiers surrounding the group. Finally, looking at the fat man, she spoke slowly, feeling her way. 'You understand, Mr. Soldier, excuse us ...'

'Soldier? Shit! Sergeant!'

'Huh? And a sergeant isn't a soldier?'

'Enough of that, dammit! I'm just about to lose my patience. What the hell kind of nonsense is this?'

Looking towards Zefa and Bina to see that they were approving her words, Grandma told about all the confusion of the hen and the egg and why they were fighting. The sergeant, amused now, also looked at the women's faces to uncover the truth of all this, suspicious that they were trying to fool him.

'And your men, where are they?'

It was *nga* Bina who answered first, saying her man was in

jail and she wanted the egg, pregnant like she was she had a great craving for it. But the sergeant didn't pay her any attention; he shook his head, then muttered, 'In jail, eh! Probably a terrorist. And the hen?'

Every head turned towards the corner under the *mandioqueiras* where the boys, squatting around the basket, were guarding Cabiri. One soldier ignored *nga* Zefa's protests and the objections of her friends and went over to the corner. He placed his hand under the basket, grabbed the hen by her wings and brought her like that to the sergeant. Cabiri didn't even squawk, but her eyes, wide with fear, looked at her friends Beto and Xico sitting sadly in the corner. The sergeant also grabbed her by the wings and leaned her against his fat belly. He spat and turning to the waiting women – *nga* Zefa's heart was beating like a drum, Bina was laughing inside – he spoke, 'Since you didn't come to any conclusion about the hen and the egg, I'll resolve it!'

He laughed, his small eyes almost disappearing into the middle of the fat of his cheeks, then winking at his assistants he shouted, 'You were disturbing the public order in this yard, you noisy gossips! More than two people were together here, that's prohibited! And furthermore, with this crazy idea of deciding your own disputes you were trying to take justice into your own hands! The hen goes with me as evidence and you start moving! Let's go, circulate! Go on home!'

The eager soldiers began to swing their white clubs over their heads. Many fled immediately, but *nga* Zefa, accustomed to fighting, refused to let her hen go just like that to some soldier's barbecue like these patrol men wanted. She threw herself on the sergeant, trying to grab the hen, but he pushed her away, raising the creature high above his head where the frightened Cabiri began to squawk, shaking her fat body and scratching his arm with her claws.

'Ay, ay, ay! Calm down, little woman! Otherwise you'll go to jail. Now take it easy!'

But at that moment while *nga* Zefa was trying to take the hen from the fat sergeant, amusing Grandma Bebeca, *nga* Bina and the others who had stayed, something close to magic happened and caused confusion everywhere.

When the soldier had gone to take the hen from under the basket, Beto and Xico were looking quietly at each other and if the people had paid any attention to that look they would have seen straight away that not even soldiers could frighten or defeat the children of the *musseque*. Beto whispered to Xico, 'Listen, Xico. These men aren't going to take Cabiri away just like that! We have to fight them in our own way!'

'Let's go, Beto! Fast!'

'No, you stay. To fool them.'

And Beto, just like a cat, slid his thin body through the hole in the planks of the fence and disappeared, running behind *sô* Zé's *quitanda*. Xico stuck out his ears in concentration, waiting for the signal which would save Cabiri. And it was that sound which dumbfounded the people while the sergeant was trying to keep the hen away from the long skinny arms of *nga* Zefa.

It was actually almost five-thirty, the sun was shining brightly and night was still a long way off. Even if it had got cooler; but no, in spite of the breeze, the *musseque* had not yet lost the thick and heavy heat of the day. How could a rooster at that hour start singing so happily and contentedly his song for wooing the hens? Everyone was amazed and even Cabiri stopped moving, except for swinging her head all around, rolling her eyes, searching in the wind for that familiar song which was calling her, telling her her mate had found an insect to eat or a good spot to take a dirt bath. Louder than all the other sounds came that fresh, pretty, trusting song from somewhere near *sô* Zé's shop of a rooster challenging Cabiri.

And then it happened. Cabiri dug her nails into the sergeant's arm, making deep scratches, then flapped her wings with all her might and the clapping, whooping, laughing, jeering women saw the fat hen soar off above the yard, straight and light and fast just like a bird that had been flying forever. And since it was already five-thirty and there wasn't even one cloud in the blue sky where it met the sea, also blue and brilliant, when they all tried to follow Cabiri's flight in the direction of the sun, they suddenly saw the creature become black in the middle and red on the sides and then disappear in the flame of the sun's rays ...

With their hands over their eyes which hurt from that brightness, the sergeant and soldiers left grumbling over the lost chance of a free barbecued chicken. The women watched them with taunting eyes, the girls laughed. The wind slowly began to blow the leaves of the *mandioqueira* trees. *Nga* Zefa felt her breast light and empty and a nice warmth filled her whole body because right in the middle of the rooster's crowing she knew it was coming from her yard, she knew the voice of her son, that little mischief-maker could imitate the talk of creatures and fool them. She called to Xico and caressing the *monandengue*'s hair, she spoke in a friendly way to her neighbours, laughing, 'It was Beto! He really sounded like a rooster. I bet Cabiri's already in the coop!'

Grandma Bebeca also laughed. Holding the egg in her dry hand, full of the lines of her years, she gave it to Bina. 'Can I, Zefa?'

Embarrassed, Beto's mother didn't want to free the smile that was playing on her face. To hide her smile she simply began by saying, 'Sure, Grandma! ... it's the pregnancy. Those cravings, I know ... Besides the child in her belly cries out for it.'

Holding the egg in her hand, Bina smiled. Slowly and tenderly the wind blew her worn dress against her young body. As it dropped down into the sea, the sun left red sparkles on the gentle waves of the bay. To all of them and in the surprised *monandengue* eyes of the child Xico, *nga* Bina's firm round belly beneath the dress seemed like it was a big, big, big egg ...

*   *   *

My tale.

If it's pretty, if it's ugly, only you know. But I swear I didn't tell a lie and that these affairs happened in this our land of Luanda.

Luanda, 1963

GLOSSARY

aiuê	Kimbundu; exclamation of pain or anguish.
aka	Kimbundu; exclamation of amazement or alarm.
ambul'o kuku	Kimbundu; 'let the old man go'.
assimilado	Portuguese; 'assimilated'; in Portugal's African colonies the assimilated status was conferred upon an African or *mestiço* (mulatto) who could prove mastery of the Portuguese language and culture. By 1961, when the assimilated status was legally abolished, less than one per cent of Angolan Africans had this status which made them juridically, but not in practice, equal to a Portuguese citizen.
auá	Kimbundu; exclamation of surprise or doubt.
azulinho	Portuguese; diminutive of *azul* (blue), i.e. 'little blue'.
bitacaia	Portuguese corruption of Kimbundu *ditacaia* (plural is *matacaia*, spelled *matacanha* in Portuguese). It is a flea which usually attacks the extremities. As it burrows into the flesh it leaves a sack of eggs (see *mauindo*). If left unattended or if poorly treated, the eggs hatch and the new fleas spread. In the worst cases the

new fleas can eat away the flesh of the feet, for instance, until gangrene sets in and destroys them.

cacimbo

Portuguese; in Angola *cacimbo* is the period of the year, generally May to mid-August, when days are cool, overcast, or foggy though not rainy, and nights are foggy or misty with a heavy dew.

candingolo

Kimbundu (or Umbundu, language of the Ovimbundu people of central Angola); home-made liquor made from sugar.

C.F.B. (Caminho de Ferro de Benguela)

Portuguese; the Benguela Railway which runs 840 miles east–west across the centre of Angola.

cipaio

Portuguese; 'sepoy'. In Angola the *cipaio* was a black police assistant under the colonial civil administration. He was often used by the higher authorities to administer corporal punishment to Africans or in the forced searches of the *musseques* that went on during the war of liberation. For these and other reasons, the *cipaio* was generally hated by the African population.

compadre

Portuguese; literally *compadre* (co-father) described the relationship between a father and the godfather of his child; figuratively, among Angola's African population this term came to be used for very close friends, whether or not the godfather relationship existed between them.

Coqueiros

Portuguese; literally *coqueiro* is the coconut palm tree; in the city of

111

Luanda, *Coqueiros* is the name of its oldest neighbourhood.

diamba   Kimbundu; 'marijuana' (also called *liamba*).

elá   Kimbundu; exclamation of surprise or dismay.

ená   Kimbundu; exclamation of surprise.

escudo   Portuguese; monetary unit used in Angola before independence. At the time this story was written, one *escudo* was roughly equal to $0.035.

Florestas   Portuguese; literally 'forests'; in Luanda of the 1940s *Florestas* was the name of a heavily wooded area on the outskirts of the city which became a natural park.

Francês-1   Portuguese; brand name of an inexpensive non-filter cigarette in Angola.

Gágá   Portuguese; affectionate diminutive of the name Garrido.

gumbatete   Kimbundu; literally 'mason'; also the name given to a yellow and black builder-wasp which uses mud to build its nest.

Hengele   Kimbundu; proper name meaning 'wit'.

Icolibengo   Portuguese: *Icolo e Bengo*; Kimbundu: *Ikolo ia Mbengu*; a geographical region north of Luanda known to the Portuguese authorities as a centre of strong nationalist sentiments and activities (specifically of the Movement for the Liberation of Angola, MPLA). It was the birthplace of Dr. Antonio Agostinho Neto, leader of the MPLA during the war of liberation and Angola's first President after independence.

imbondeiro	Portuguese; 'baobub' tree common throughout much of Angola. *Imbondeiro* originates from the Kimbundu word for the baobub, *mbondo*.
jindungo	Kimbundu; 'hot red pepper' (called *piri-piri* in Portuguese).
jinguba	Kimbundu; 'peanut'.
jinguna	Kimbundu; a kind of winged white ant or termite which comes out of the ground after a rainfall.
Kabulu	Kimbundu; literally 'rabbit'. In the first story it is the name of a popular song. In the second story it is the nickname given to this particular white man, the implication being that the man is clever since in popular lore the rabbit is thought of as a clever animal.
Kam'tuta	Kimbundu; *mututa* means 'masturbation' or 'sodomy'; the prefix *ka* in Kimbundu implies a nickname.
katul'o maku	Kimbundu; 'take your hands off'.
Kimbundu	language spoken by the Mbundu people who live in and around the provinces of Luanda, Malange, Kwanza-Norte and Kwanza-Sul.
Kinaxixi	Kimbundu; name of a public square near the centre of Luanda and of the large public market located along one side of this square.
Kuanza	Kimbundu; name of large river which forms the southern boundary of the province of Luanda; also spelled *Kwanza*.
Lixeira	Portuguese; literally 'rubbish dump'; name of a *musseque* in Luanda located on

	the site of the city's former rubbish dump.
Luuanda	Kimbundu pronunciation of Angola's capital city Luanda.
Madia	Kimbundu pronunciation of the name Maria.
mandioqueira	Portuguese; 'matchwood' tree commonly found in the tiny back yards of the *musseques*.
maquezo	Portuguese spelling of Kimbundu *makezu*; cola nuts with a little ginger sprinkled on top.
Marçal	Portuguese; name of a *musseque* in Luanda.
massuícas	Portuguese spelling of Kimbundu *masuika*; a group of three large stones put together for use as a hearth for cooking.
matete	Kimbundu; porridge or gruel made from manioc or maize flour.
matias	Portuguese; a bird whose name in Kimbundu, *mbolo-kinhentu*, imitates the sound of the bird's song and means 'five-penny-bread'.
mauindo	Portuguese spelling of Kimbundu *mauindu*; the sack of eggs made by the *bitacaia* flea.
Mbaxi	Kimbundu; proper name, equivalent of the Portuguese name Sebastião.
Mbengu	Kimbundu; name of large river which forms the northern boundary of the province of Luanda, called Bengo by the Portuguese.
m'bika a mundele, mundele uê	Kimbundu; 'the servant of a white man is also white'.

114

mona	Kimbundu; 'child' (male or female); the Portuguese plural, *monas*, means 'children'.
monandengue	Kimbundu; slight distortion of phrase *mona a ndengue*, 'young child' or, less literally, 'youngster'.
monangamba	Kimbundu; slight distortion of phrase *mona a ngamba*, used to describe a porter, carrier, loader, or servant whose work involves heavy manual labour. By extension this term was also used to describe Africans recruited for forced labour.
mulemba	Kimbundu; a kind of sycamore tree common throughout Luanda.
musseque	Kimbundu; originated from the phrase *ngoloia mu seke* (I'm going where the earth is clay-like). *Seke* designated the coarse rust-coloured sand good for growing manioc which could be found throughout the city of Luanda. As more and more people came to the capital, the manioc crops disappeared and in their place thousands of shanties sprang up which sheltered these poor newcomers to the city. During the 1950s and 1960s and until independence, *musseque* implied the urban African ghetto (or slum) in Angola. See *Preface*.
Mutamba	Kimbundu; a main square in Downtown (the centre of) Luanda which was also the main bus stop for the Africans who worked in the city but lived in the *musseques*.
mutopa	Kimbundu; a kind of water pipe attached to a gourd.

Naxinha	Portuguese; affectionate diminutive of name Inácia.
nga	Kimbundu; 'Mr.' or 'Mrs.'; abbreviation of *ngana*, 'Mister' or 'Missus'.
ngoma	Kimbundu; 'drum'. This particular drum is commonly used in the small bands popular at parties in the *musseque*.
ngueta	Kimbundu; pejorative term for a white man.
piápia	Kimbundu; 'swallow'; in Portuguese the plural is *piápias*.
pírula	Kimbundu; a bird common in the province of Luanda which is known to sing sadly when the weather is rainy or overcast. According to Vieira it looks something like a kingfisher. In Portuguese the plural is *pírulas*.
plim-plau	Portuguese; a greyish songbird common in the province of Luanda.
polo-ia-hima	Kimbundu; 'monkey-face'.
quimbombo	Portuguese spelling of Kimbundu *kimbombo*; home-made liquor made from corn or manioc flour.
quiqüerra	Portuguese; a sweet made from shredded and toasted manioc flour mixed with sugar and peanuts.
quissonde	Portuguese spelling of Kimbundu *kisonde*; red ant which inflicts a painful bite.
quitanda	Portuguese spelling of Kimbundu *kitanda*; small shop, a few of which also serve meals and drinks.
quitande	Portuguese spelling of Kimbundu *kitande*; raw dried beans which have been soaked in water and their skins re-

116

	moved then cooked up with palm oil to make a stew.
rabo–de–junco	Portuguese; greyish songbird found in the province of Luanda.
Rangel	Portuguese; name of a *musseque* in Luanda.
Sambizanga	Kimbundu; name of a *musseque* in Luanda.
sô, sôr	Portuguese; corruption of *senhor*, 'mister'.
sukua'	Kimbundu; abbreviation of *sukuama*.
sukuama	Kimbundu; exclamation of disgust, anger, or surprise.
uatobaram	Kimbundu/Portuguese; third–person plural, present tense, of verb *uatobar* which is a 'portuguesation' of the Kimbundu verb *ku toba* ('to act foolishly' or 'to say foolish things'). By extension the verb also describes the act of children who clap their hands against their mouths while yelling *uatobo, uatobo*, meaning 'you fool, you fool'.
uazekele kié–uazeka kiambote	Kimbundu; 'how are you, are you well?'
Ximba Ximba não usa cuecas	Kimbundu; insulting name for a *cipaio*. Kimbundu and Portuguese; '*Ximba* doesn't wear underpants.' This was a traditional insult for a *cipaio* because while the *cipaio* was given a kind of uniform by the authorities, that uniform did not include underwear.

Mu muhatu mu 'mbia! Mu tunda uazele, mu tunda uaxikelela, mu tunda uakusuka ...
Kimbundu; 'A woman is like a pot! Out of her can come something white, something black, something red ...'

mu 'xi ietu iá Luuanda mubita ima ikuata sonii ...
Kimbundu; 'in this our land of Luanda painful things are happening'.

... ngala ngó ku kakela/ká ... ká ... ká ... kakela, kakela ...
Kimbundu; 'All I'm doing is cackling/ca ca ca cackling, cackling ...'

Ngëxile kua ngana Zefa/Ngala ngó ku kakela/Ká ... ká ... ká ... kakela, kakela ...
Kimbundu; 'I went to the house of Missus Zefa/All I'm doing is cackling/Ca ... ca ... ca ... cackling, cackling ...'

... ngëjile kua ngana Bina/Ala kiá ku kuata/kua ... kua ... kua ... kuata, kuata!
Kimbundu; 'I came to the house of Missus Bina/Already they are grabbing/grab ... grab ... grab ... grabbing, grabbing!'